PRINCE'S TIDE

M.L. EADEN

Copyright © 2023 by M.L. Eaden

All rights reserved.

No portion of this book may be reproduced in any form without written permission from the publisher or author, except as permitted by U.S. copyright law.

Edited By Victoria Flickinger: flickeringwords.com

Cover Art By Hollyanne Hook: etsy.com/shop/SupernaturalByHolly

Print ISBN: **978-1-956128-29-1**   EBook ISBN: **978-1-956128-28-4**

Published in cooperation with Chaotic Neutral Press LLC.

Content Warnings: Explicit on-page sex. Capture, torture, imprisonment by antagonist, teratophilia.

PRINCE'S TIDE

Mythical Desires Universe

By M.L. Eaden

Queer Stories based in myth, legend, and the uniquely mundane.

CONTENTS

1. Once Upon A Time — 1
2. Two Legs — 7
3. The Redhead — 12
4. Communication — 16
5. Explanations Needed — 21
6. Sweet Tooth — 26
7. Braids — 31
8. Out & About — 36
9. Dead Things — 43
10. Anticipation — 49
11. Conundrum — 54
12. Clarity — 59
13. Oh For Pete's Sake — 64
14. The Gulf — 69
15. Coastal Waters — 76
16. Like Royalty — 84
17. Anatomy Lesson — 90
18. New Season — 97

19.	Learning Curve	106
20.	The Blue Dress	110
21.	Healing Touch	120
22.	Perfect Storm	127
23.	Woven Reeds & Words	136
24.	Torn Loyalties	140
25.	Sacrifices	146
26.	Overwhelmed	153
27.	Hallucinations	159
28.	Thin Patience	167
29.	A Relative Problem	173
30.	Marking Time	179
31.	Moment Of Truth	183
32.	Test Of Wills	189
33.	Yearend Feast	193
34.	The Lost	198
35.	Lover's Marks	205
36.	Inheritance	212
37.	Stasis	216
38.	Guardians	221
39.	Safe Harbor	231
40.	Traps	236
41.	Old Friends	243
42.	Coming Home	253

43. We Are Family 257
44. Epilogue Of Pete 263

Once Upon A Time

Royce

"Once upon a time, right?" I chuckled. "That's how most fairy tales start. Mine's no different." The crew were mostly greenhorns, finishing their first season. Kristy and Pete were the only ones that had been with me longer, and Pete had been on my boat for almost a decade now. Tonight was for teaching the greenhorns how to tell tall tales—and drinking. "It's a long tradition and I have one, if you're willing to listen."

It was the whiskey talking, mostly. I knew that, yet I couldn't help myself. My crew was sitting around a table we had commandeered, most of them drunk, too.

"About this time last year," I started, "I was sitting in this very bar, sipping my drink, wondering if I should retire. See, something strange happened to me a week before, not far off of San José Island, when I was securing the boat. A trapline or rigging, not sure which, hit me and I was thrown overboard."

I continued the story to their rapt attention. The sounds of the bar around us faded into the background. Logan's Pub, named after the guy that first started the place, or a legend, no one was really sure, had that evening air of mystery with low lighting and hushed conversations. A storm was coming in, and everyone who had a boat in port was here waiting it out.

"I was alone on deck. Our vigilant first mate, old Pete over there—" Pete was trying to hide his red-faced embarrassment in his beer. His ears were pink, and his brown hair and red beard didn't help the situation. Some of the crew chuckled.

"He left me all by my lonesome." There were appropriate hisses and boos in recognition of the safety issue.

We had caught little that week, and the crew wanted to go ashore for a night. Kristy had volunteered to take the group to Port Aransas, which wasn't too far away. I let them take the tender while Pete and I kept an eye on the boat. It didn't hurt that we had traps set in the area. We were trying a long soak and planned to pick them up later, hoping we'd increase our catch.

"You left him alone, Pete?" one of the crew asked.

"Marcy called." More groans from the crew. They all knew how badly he had it for the local baker. "I didn't expect him to keep working without me. He knows better." He pointed a finger at me as he finished his beer. "So don't groan at me."

It definitely wasn't his fault. I should have waited for him to come back, but when he gets to talking with Marcy, it could be ten minutes or two hours. I continued my story as if I wasn't interrupted.

"I, being your fearless and careless captain, saw a loose rig and thought I would fix it up right quick." Thinking about what happened that night still scared me. I took a drink to help steady my voice. "But the boat shifted, and something hit me. I was in the water before I could think to call out or yell." I knew how to swim, but at night it was hard to tell which way was up.

"Right then and there, I knew I was going to die, and I stopped fighting the sea. I figured if this was the cost of twenty years of prosperity for me, my crew, and my family, I'd pay it."

"What happened next, Captain?" Kristy asked. She was our second, training to take over from Pete or me, depending on how things shook out. Tonight, her hair was free of its usual tight braids, her dark brown eyes alight with interest. Even dressed in overalls, work boots, and a tank top, she had her pick of admirers.

"Well, once you decide to stop fighting, the sea either takes you or throws you out." I took another drink. I was fairly sure they would think it was a drinking story, which was fine by me. I almost didn't believe it myself. "Instead, it sent me the most handsome face I'd ever seen, attached to a swimmer's body with fins. They grabbed me by the collar and hauled me up to the surface. Next thing I knew, I was staring into their face. They had black orbs for eyes, but they weren't unkind. They reminded me of the sea on a moonless night. I gasped for breath as we held onto a trap buoy close to the boat."

No one said anything. A few looked surprised. Others took pulls from their drinks. No one checked their phones, though they were all in plain sight on the table. My drink made me brave enough to talk. Only the sea knows why.

"I had no idea where they came from, or why they had bothered to drag me to the surface. Their webbed, taloned hand reached to touch my face." I mimicked the motion. Every pair of eyes followed my hand as if they were seeing it for themselves. "Their hand slid across my jaw in a curious manner, like they'd never seen a beard. They had none themselves, though the hair on their head was red as blood and their skin was blue, I can't quite describe." The light from the boat had flashed across their hair and skin, showing the rich colors.

"I hacked up a lung as they watched." I thought about that night. He could have left me on that buoy, but he stayed and watched while I tried to breathe air again.

"We both flinched at a whistle. I remember because the sudden sound hurt my ears. And the creature opened their mouth full of pointed teeth and snarled. Then they turned away from me, as quick as a seal, and dove back into the dark water they came from. I haven't seen anything like them since."

"Do you look for them?" someone asked. I was too busy staring into my glass to know who it was for sure, but it sounded like Chris.

"No, I mean, who knows if they're real or if I made them up to explain what happened?" The water can do strange things at night, and it was easier to think I imagined it all.

"Pete found me and hauled my ass on board. I took ill from the experience. When the crew got back to the boat, we picked up the traps and headed to Galveston. We've been around San José Island since then, and so have others. No one has seen anything like it. Hell, there aren't even stories about merfolk in that area." I should know. I checked in every port we stopped in and asked around.

"So," Jamie said, "you're telling us a merfolk rescued you, and that's why you didn't retire last season?" She gave me a curious look, obviously dubious of my choice, my story, or both.

"Yep." I finished my drink and set the glass down. "I thought about it, but I figured if the sea didn't want me, and the merfolk went to all the trouble of saving me, maybe I should keep doing what I'm good at, you know?"

"Ahhhhh, you salty dog, you're still looking for them," Kristy said, her eyes full of mirth.

"Nah," I replied. "I know better than to ask for lightning to strike twice. Besides, I'm pretty sure I hallucinated all of it. I had a pretty good knock on the head from the gear."

The crew were shaking their heads. Pete spoke up. "Here's to the Captain! Too salty for the sea, too in love with it to let it go."

"Here! Here!" We drank some more. The crew told more stories, racier than the one I told. Eventually, I begged off and left for the dock. The *Aire Apparent* sat high on its metal composite hull in the harbor after its holding tanks were flushed. The gangway rocked as the wind picked up. Muscle memory took over as I swayed up the zipper-shaped structure to the main deck. I barely made it to my quarters as the first thunder boomed from the storm blowing in.

I watched through a port window as a flash streaked the sky. Another flash followed and lit up the window like a mirror. In it, I saw a figure standing in my cabin doorway. I had to be seeing things from the drink. I rubbed my eyes, sure of it, until I turned and the figure was still there.

They were naked and gasping as if they'd run a kilometer or more. Not a word was uttered as they placed one shaky foot into my cabin. I moved forward to meet them, prepared for a fight if necessary. Much to my surprise, they fell into my arms.

Their dark red hair, draped over their shoulders, glistened in the hallway light. The handsome individual shivered in my arms, clearly cold, and possibly fighting off shock. I set them on my bunk and fought my brain fog to take the steps necessary to help them. I closed my cabin door, stripped out of my clothing down to my underwear, grabbed blankets from my storage chest, and wrapped us up together in my bunk. We didn't speak as the other pressed into me and eventually stopped shivering, then fell deep asleep.

Talking about the merfolk and too much drink had me thinking it was a dream until I woke up the next morning with a headache, a hard-on, and a very naked person sleeping in my arms.

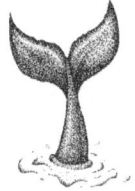

TWO LEGS

Troller

The warmth I was wrapped in suddenly disappeared, as if something had lifted me out of the ocean and left me to dry. I shivered and grasped blindly for the large cloth and the human that had been with me. It was too bright to open my eyes and the smallest movement incited pain. Cramps shot up from my fin. No, not fin, feet. Legs. After so long searching, I couldn't believe I found the boat and the human I rescued.

Born of desperation, I left everything I knew in search of the human I had saved and his ship. When I found the boat again, I was elated. So many shifts of the current and turns of the moon had passed, searching harbors and ports for the boat under the cover of night. I found a spot near the dock where the boat was moored, and watched it for any signs of the one I rescued. By the laws of the sea, he owed me his life. If he was still associated with the vessel he had fallen from, I would board it and ask for my favor. All I needed was a place to shelter so I could plan, then return to my pod.

Late into the night, I saw the human. He was much larger than I realized. He thundered up the planks and onto the vessel, grunting as he went.

The sight of him warmed my insides, though thoughts of asking for the favor he owed me fled. His facial hair and well-muscled arms were the same as I remembered. He reminded me of the protectors of our pods. Or a very cranky slickfur, making honking barks from shore before they dove into the water. Perhaps he was injured. It was hard to tell with humans. He hadn't yelled when he fell. If I could help him again, another favor would be owed.

Determined and emboldened by the possibility, I launched myself out of the water and grabbed onto a rope that hung from the side of the boat. As I pulled myself up and onto the deck, a wild wind kicked up and the storm that had held off for most of the night started in earnest.

Once I was on the boat, I began my change. I braced for the excruciating pain, expecting the same abrasive sensations as I felt on the beach after the first time. However, the surface under my hands had a worn texture that offered better purchase and was more gentle than sand to my newly formed skin. I watched as the eddies of water on the deck picked up the evidence of my other self. It carried the remnants of my luminescent scales and powerful fins over the side of the boat.

Without my protective skin, I shivered. I had not anticipated the thermal difference of the chilly rain on my new surface dweller skin. Seeking cover, I crawled toward what looked like an opening. My newly formed legs protested as I levered myself up and opened the barrier that kept me from finding shelter. The surface dweller tendency to block paths, even on their vessels, had always seemed odd to me, and now it served as an annoyance keeping me from my goal. Everything blurred and my eyes burned while my vision adjusted. I stumbled down a narrow passage until I heard breathing. I followed the sound until it brought me to a living space where the large beautiful human stood gazing out the window at the storm.

The lightning put his form in relief, outlining his head of black hair, shoulders, and arms. When he turned to find me braced against the wall, I had hoped to demand my favor. Instead, my throat seized for lack of moisture. A gasping noise came from my mouth and a moment later, I was in his arms. He touched my hair, like I'd touched his so long ago. Another wave of relief washed through me at his gentleness.

He picked me up as if I was a trout and put me on the sleeping platform. He wrapped us in cloth and wrapped his arms around me. My chill subsided, and I slept, exhausted.

The light and my muscles cramping from shifting brought me to the present. I pulled the cloth over my head and wondered why I was alone on the sleeping platform. I had my answer when the cloth was gently pulled back. I scrambled to pull it back over my head.

I heard a noise, and the light disappeared. A deep voice asked, "Better?"

I moved the cloth and looked at him. I didn't know the word, only that it was a query and answered with a nod, hoping it was the correct response. He nodded in return.

"Here, I brought you something for your stomach."

I sat up and let the cloth pool around my hips. He sat next to me and handed me a warm cup of liquid. The smell reminded me of seagulls. I took a sip and warmth shot through me, reminding me how hungry I was. I tipped the cup back gulped the hot liquid. Once I'd emptied it, I held it out to him.

The smile on his face made my heart beat faster. His kind, light brown eyes were exactly as I remembered them. His facial hair exaggerated his smile, and I risked a smile in return. He took the cup from my hand.

"Would you like more?" he asked as he pointed to the cup.

I nodded hoping he would bring me more seagull liquid. But when he stood, panic went through me as I realized he meant to leave again. I reached for his arm to stop him.

"Shit, you're strong."

I stared at him and pleaded with my brain to form a word, a sound that would make sense. "No."

"If you want more," he tapped the cup, "I have to go to the galley to get it." He pointed toward the door.

My throat was dry, but I hummed and clicked, pointing to the cup, unable to use his words.

"You want more?" He tapped the cup and mimicked drinking from it as I had done earlier. Maybe he meant to have some himself. I tried to take the cup from him and explain that he needed his own. He made a funny barking noise when I tried to communicate. My tones and clicks were lost on him.

"You sound like a dolphin, but your voice is deeper. Is that what you are?"

It was another query. I was growing tired of them. I reached for the cup and this time he let me have it. He pointed at it, then his mouth, without saying more words I didn't understand. This time I nodded, and he left without the cup.

I knew there was a separate space for food. I've seen enough ships and shipwrecks to know that. He only had cloth covering his hips and legs, and he wore coverings on his feet. They squeaked as he walked. I had no coverings except the cloth I had slept in. The soft keening noise I made matched my sorrow expressing how unprepared I was for this journey.

THE REDHEAD

Royce

I stood in the galley, dumbfounded. We lived in a world full of magical beings, but there were some things people thought were long extinct. Unicorns for one, and merfolk being another. No one had seen one in ages, and here I had one in my bunk. Or a dolphin shifter, but if that was the case, they might have known English or some other land based language. The redhead clearly didn't.

Maybe it was a coincidence that his hair was the same color red as the individual that rescued me. *Maybe I imagined the scales and fins. But where would he have come from? No one else was out there besides Pete and me.*

"You're going to drive yourself into an aneurysm thinking like this," I muttered to myself as I heated more broth. I filled another cup and went back to my room.

He was still sitting up, which was a good sign. His hair was matted, and I noticed a couple of cuts on both sides of his neck and torso near his ribs, but they looked scabbed over. I handed over the cup, exchanging it for the empty one. He nodded and raised the cup in what seemed to be a gesture of gratitude.

"You're welcome." I walked three paces back to my desk, sat at my desk chair, and watched as he drank his second helping a little slower this time.

"Do you have a name?" He glanced at me but continued to drink. "Nombre?" I asked. My Spanish was horrible, but that didn't seem to spark any kind of recognition, either.

"Royce," I said as I pointed to myself. If that didn't work, I could make up a name for him.

He nodded and patted his chest. "Troller."

"Hmmm. Okay." He pronounced it as troll-er. It reminded me of trolling, which was an old form of fishing where the boat moved slowly and dragged fishing lines behind it. It wasn't as sustainable as trap fishing and eventually it, and trawling with nets, were phased out.

He looked at me with a blank expression. Yeah, just my luck that trying to communicate wouldn't be easy. The tablet I used to track things for the boat and my business was on my desk. I grabbed it and moved to sit next to him. I searched for a language app, then realized that wouldn't work. Whatever his language was to begin with, it wasn't likely to be anything current. I opened my e-reader instead and loaded several children's books with read-along functionality. I held out my hand for his empty cup. He gave it to me, and I set it aside, then put the tablet in his hands.

"Okay, let's see what you can do with this." I showed him the motions to turn pages and sat with him as he went through the first book. He stopped on the letter P and looked at me.

"Pants." He pointed to the one article of clothing I wore, then pointed to himself. "Pants," he repeated.

"Fuck, right. Maybe I can pilfer something from Pete's locker. You're about his size." As I stood, Troller didn't stop me. Engrossed with the images from the book, he only glanced at me as I left the room.

When I came back from grabbing some of Pete's clothes, Troller was animated. He pulled me through the door and excitedly pointed at things. I tried to ignore the fact that he was naked and kept my eyes above his waist.

"Desk!" Troller pointed. "Pencil. Cup. Chair. Bed. Blanket. Book." I nodded as he displayed how fast he learned.

"Shirt," I said as I tossed it at him. "Pants." I tossed him the pair I had found.

He caught the items and looked them over. "Shirt. Pants," he repeated. He looked at me as he stood there holding them.

It dawned on me that he probably knew what clothes were, though if this was his first time on land, he wouldn't know what to do with them. I thanked myself for grabbing gray sweatpants instead of a pair of Pete's jeans.

He didn't shy away from me as I moved toward him. I took the shirt from his hands and bunched it up, then pulled it over his head. I helped guide one arm through a sleeve, then repeated it with the other. He smiled as he looked at what he wore. The T-shirt had a band logo on it. It wasn't fancy, but it hugged his chest like a second skin and highlighted the fact that he was nude from the waist down.

As I picked up the sweatpants from where he had dropped them, I cleared my throat and crouched down, bunching up the legs. He instinctively put his hand on my shoulder as I reached for his left leg and put one foot through, then repeated the same motion with the other. I grabbed the elastic of the waistband and pulled them up his legs, holding it open wide enough that I wouldn't brush against his groin too much, then pulled them to his waist. He grasped my forearms as I used the strings to cinch and tie the pants so they wouldn't fall off.

Troller and Pete were pretty close in size, though Troller's waist was slightly smaller and he was more toned versus the muscles Pete sported in his upper body. Though Troller had abs and a defined chest with nipples. Why would a merfolk have nipples? I was distracted by the odd thought until I heard Troller's voice.

"Thanks," Troller said, in a quiet tenor that made me smile.

"You're welcome."

He slowly let go of my arms and sat on the platform. After holding him most of the night and being close now, I hadn't realized how much I wanted to touch him again. I picked up the device and handed it back to him. He took it and curled up on the bed, legs tucked to the side, and bowed his head in concentration. I listened for a moment as he heard the words and repeated them back to the device.

I took the empty cups and went back to the galley to make myself some coffee, then check the boat to see if there was any damage from last night's storm. I probably had a goofy grin on my face the whole time. It was tempered with questions about where Troller had come from and why he had shown up almost a year after he rescued me. If he actually was the same individual that rescued me the night I almost died. I had no way of knowing for sure until we figured out how to communicate in more than one-word sentences, though I believed in my gut it was him.

COMMUNICATION

Troller

The device Royce gave me helped immensely. My vocabulary expanded in a matter of hours. I recognized the words, as we have many examples of surface dweller writings from their discarded and lost detritus. The only thing I had lacked to understand them were the sounds. Even with what I knew, I hadn't realized there were so many things to learn. Royce came to check on me as he went about his day. It displeased me when he took the device out of my hand.

"Please, Royce, give it back," I pleaded. His eyes were wide and his mouth hung slightly open. Then he gave me a beautiful smile. The warmth it created in me was pleasing, though he kept the device from me.

"You're learning pretty quickly, but you need to take a break. You've been at it for eight hours. Are you hungry?"

"Yes." I thought about it more and my stomach grumbled its own answer. "Yes, Royce, I am hungry." I unfolded my legs, pushed up from the bed, and immediately fell forward. Royce caught me as I tried to find my balance, my legs protesting the movement.

"Take it slow." He put his arm around my waist and helped me maneuver from his room, then stood behind me with his hands on my hips and my hands braced on the walls as we moved down the walkway to the food area.

"What would you like to eat?" Royce sat me at the little table in the corner, then moved about the room again as I watched. "We don't have much to choose from right now since I haven't restocked yet. The season's ended, so the normal supplies won't be in for a few months. But I can go to the store tomorrow and get what we need."

I understood about half of what he said, so I focused on the question. "I eat fish. Crab. Seaweed. Snails. Lobster. Seagulls. It was the soup, yes?"

He gave me a curious look and replied, "Ah, no, that was synthetic protein broth. It's supposed to taste like chicken, not seagulls, but I guess they might be similar."

"Oh, chicken. Land bird. I remember. It was good."

"I'm glad you liked it," Royce said with a smile. "How about we try a sandwich?"

"I know this word, but why would one eat sand? The picture was not sand."

Royce laughed. "Well, it's not made of sand, it's made of bread. Have you had bread before?"

"No." I was curious. I had seen a picture, but we had nothing like that where I came from.

Royce paused for a moment. "Well," he started, then stopped and looked at me. "Maybe it would be better if I showed you."

I watched as Royce spread thick substances on squares of sponge that didn't look edible. He squished two pieces together and then two more. When he came to the table, he brought the sponges with the substances on a plate. He returned to the preparation area and retrieved two cups with a white substance he had poured into both.

I wasn't sure what to do with them. Royce noticed and helpfully demonstrated. "Here, like this." He took a bite, and I watched as he chewed. To say it fascinated me would be an understatement. I picked up my sandwich and mirrored Royce's actions.

I'd never tasted anything like it. It was soft, sweet, and sticky. It was wonderful, and it stuck to the roof of my mouth. I spent a moment savoring the bite I'd taken before I swallowed. "What is this? Do all sandwiches taste like this?"

Royce's smile made my skin flush with a pink color. He wasn't cruel when he answered my questions. Our elders had told us surface dwellers were cruel. Royce continued to prove them wrong.

"No, there are different kinds. This is a peanut butter and jelly sandwich." He opened his two pieces and showed me the substances. "This is peanut butter, and this is strawberry jam. You put them on bread," he pointed to the things I had thought were an edible sponge, "and they make a sandwich."

"Oh. It is good." I took another bite as I watched Royce drink some of the white liquid substance from a cup. I stopped eating the sandwich enough to ask about the liquid. "What is this?"

"Milk."

"Milk, Royce?"

"Do you want to try it?"

I nodded and picked up the cup in front of me. I took a sip and the sour sweetness didn't agree with me, but it made the sandwich pieces softer, easier to eat. I tried again, and it was easier to drink, but I preferred the protein soup.

"Do you like it?"

I shook my head and took another drink. Royce laughed. "You don't have to drink it if you don't like it."

We ate in silence for a while. When Royce was done, he wiped his face with a cloth. This action perplexed me. I took the cloth in front of me and did the same thing, which made Royce smile.

"Here, let me help. Like this," he said as he leaned toward me. His hand went to the back of my neck and gently held it as he swiped the cloth at the corners of my mouth. I felt it pull slightly and realized that I had the sticky substances on my face. "There."

I tried to smile, but didn't feel it. With each thing he helped me with, I felt a sense of exhilaration, but there was also the shame of not understanding. This was the longest I'd spent out of the water, and I had so much to learn.

"Royce."

"Yes, Troller?"

It embarrassed me to ask, but I knew the surface dwellers were different. I'd seen many relieve themselves of all kinds of things from the side of a boat. I didn't want to use the side of the boat, but I would if I had to. I stood and looked around. There was a basin nearby. I slowly moved toward it and fumbled with my pants. Royce approached before I could lower them enough to relieve myself, and he touched my arm gently.

"No, no, don't do that here. Let me show you." He offered his hand. I took it and he brought me back to his room and opened a small closet. He opened the lid of what looked like a bucket bolted to the floor. The basin from the other room was higher. This floor bucket would be easier to use.

He showed me the sink device along with the toilet device. "This is a toilet. You relieve yourself into it. It can also handle other kinds of waste. Then you press this handle when you're done, and wash your hands in the sink."

"Where does it go?" It seemed everything went down a hole. I wondered if it went directly into the water.

"It flushes to storage, which we use as fuel for the boat."

"Your waste makes the boat go?"

"Yeah. It's a clever system some technomage designed. A lot of vehicles use it, though on land they have stations that distribute the fuel."

I nodded, but only understood a small fraction of what he'd said. He stood there, and I pulled at my pants, which startled him. He moved so I could reach the floor bucket that fueled the boat.

"Sorry. I'll leave you to it. I need to clean the galley anyway." He left, and I was alone in the small room, staring at the bucket.

When I was done, I pressed the handle, and my waste disappeared. Why did people use the side of the boat if these things were available? I washed my hands and dried them, as Royce had shown me. When I left the small room, I saw the device and returned to my studies. I must have fallen asleep at some point because I woke later with a blanket wrapped around me. The only thing missing from the night before was Royce.

EXPLANATIONS NEEDED

ROYCE

When Pete nudged me awake the next morning, I realized I was still in the captain's chair. I hadn't planned on falling asleep, but it seemed prudent to stay up here given the man that was in my bunk. He had fallen asleep studying, and I covered him before I returned to the nest.

"You slept here the whole night?" Pete asked.

"Uh, yeah."

"Why?" He looked at the instrument panels, checking various systems. "Did something happen?"

"You could say that. How's Marcy?" I asked Pete, trying to divert him from asking more questions I didn't want to answer. Marcy was his current crush. She owned the bakery in town, and Pete would visit her when we were in port. To answer, Pete produced two coffees and a box of baked goods.

The scent of fresh pastries filled the nest, and my mouth watered. "If you don't marry her, I might for the baked goods alone."

Pete abruptly closed the box and moved it out of my reach. "I refuse to give you the object of your affection unless you swear right now to leave her alone."

"Do I get baked goods for life if I'm your best man?"

Pete silently handed me the box and grinned when I pulled out a bear claw. "So you are getting serious. When are you thinking about asking her?"

"Soon," Pete said, with all the hopes and dreams you could imagine wrapped up in that word. "I want it to be perfect, you know?"

"Sometimes we don't get perfect, we get a moment instead. You shouldn't wait if you're serious. Do you think she's interested?" I asked before I took a huge bite of the bear claw.

"I think so. I mean, I've caught her looking at dresses, but she tries to pretend she isn't. You know her. She's sweet, but fierce when she's upset. She has curves and an ass that won't quit. Her hair always smells like some kind of spice from her baking. With her dark brown hair and my hazel eyes, we'd make beautiful kids, I'm sure of it."

"You're a goner," I laughed. "What if they have her brown eyes?"

"Doesn't matter. So laugh all you want. If all our kids looked like her, I'd be happy. Someday you'll find someone that makes you a goner, too."

I cleared my throat. That statement hit a little too close to who was in my bunk right now.

"You didn't answer my question earlier. Why are you sleeping up here, Royce?" Pete asked again. Before I could answer, Troller appeared at the bottom of the steps to the captain's nest.

"Royce?" Troller's soft voice squeezed my heart. His long red hair was still matted, while his beautiful face held a hint of sleepiness. I couldn't speak for a moment. Pete saved me.

"Hi, I'm Pete, Royce's first mate." Pete glanced between Troller and me, then took a few steps down and held out his hand. Troller looked at Pete's hand, then me.

"He wants you to shake his hand. Come here, Pete." Pete came back up the steps and I showed him what it meant. "Like this." We shook hands and then I nodded to Pete to do the same with Troller.

When Pete went back to Troller, they shook hands, and he replied. "I am Troller. I am Royce's friend, visiting. Excuse me." Troller disappeared back down the hallway, and I got up to go after him.

"Is he wearing my clothes?" Pete asked as he came back up into the nest. I went down the stairs to find Troller. "Royce?"

"Pete, give me a minute, please." He held up his hands and shrugged.

When I opened the door, Troller sat on the bed, the tablet in his hands. He looked up and held it out to me. "It is broken, Royce. Can you fix it?"

I walked over and looked at it. It was out of power. "It needs to recharge. Maybe we can do something else today."

"What is in the box?" Troller asked.

I'd completely forgotten it was in my hands. "Pastries. Would you like one?" I opened the box and Troller's eyes lit up. "It's like bread, but different."

He took one out of the box and bit into it. His eyes widened, and he moaned. The sound hit below the belt. I tried to keep a pleasant face. "Royce, this is good! Better than the sandwich. Where do they come from?" His excitement was contagious.

"I can show you, but we should probably get you cleaned up and dressed in something better suited for going into town."

"What is wrong with my coverings?"

"They're sleeping clothes. Plus, you've worn them for a day or so. We should change them."

"Are you going to change your coverings as well?"

"Yes. After I have a shower."

"What is a shower?"

I thought about showing him exactly what a shower was, both of us naked and wet, him pressed close to me. Thankfully, my cabin shower was barely large enough for me, let alone two people, so that wasn't possible.

"I'll show you. Give me a few minutes. I need to talk with Pete." I handed Troller the box and went back to the nest. Pete gave me an amused look and my cheeks heated like I was fifteen and caught sneaking someone into my house for a make-out session.

"So, Troller, huh?" Pete asked sweetly.

"He came aboard the other night."

"And why is he wearing my clothes?"

"Because he didn't have any."

"Why did you let a naked man onto your boat?"

"Pete."

"Royce."

"It's hard to explain."

"Try me."

"It's him, Pete." I quieted my voice. "The merman that rescued me. It's him."

Pete's eyes darted from the stairs back to me and back to the stairs. He looked at me and grinned. "So it wasn't a hallucination."

"No. Seems it wasn't."

SWEET TOOTH

Troller

All the bread things Royce had handed me were marvelous, and I couldn't stop myself from eating every last one. I was so very full, and it reminded me of the last time I ate that much. It was a mid-year feast, and oysters were plentiful. The flesh was so fresh and delightful to bite into, but the memory was bittersweet. I was happy then, ignorant of everything that caused me to leave my pod behind.

There was a knock on the door. I wasn't sure why. It was odd that surface dwellers were very much about their privacy and their coverings. I opened the door and Royce stood there for a moment with more coverings in his hands.

"Pete let us borrow more clothes. We'll get you a few things when we go to town."

"Where is Pete now?" I asked, worried he might tell others I was here.

"He's seeing to the boat today."

"What is a first mate?"

"A first mate means he's next in charge of the boat after me."

Royce's mate seemed important to him, and Pete had responsibilities similar to Royce. If Royce already had a mate, would he be willing to entertain another? Sometimes waterfolk had multiple mates. Maybe surface dwellers did the same. "Do you have other mates?"

The confused look on Royce's face made my face heat. Maybe it was the wrong question to ask. His confusion changed to embarrassment as his face turned red.

"Pete and I work together. It's a job. We're friends that care about each other, that's all."

Most of the words Royce said, I understood, but I needed more information. "What does 'job' mean?"

"Well, do you perform a service or have a role where you're from?" Royce asked. He stood in front of me, holding the new coverings as he tried to explain his relationship to the other man.

I shook my head and brought my legs up to my chest. My full stomach, my memories of home, and now Royce's words made me feel alone. I couldn't tell him the truth. I wondered if this was a mistake. Maybe what little light there was the night I saw Royce's face had been a trick. Perhaps I saw things there I hadn't really understood.

"Hmm, okay, do others do things for you that are important? Like gathering food?"

"Yes. They do." I thought about that. We all took turns gathering and hunting for food. "Pete gathers food for you?"

"Uh, he helps me, and we make sure that food goes to people that give it to more people."

"Oh." There were waterfolk that had natural instincts to protect the pod and spent their lives making sure the rest of us were safe. Whether it was finding food or defending the pod from other predators, Royce reminded me of them.

From the device, I learned surface dwellers had different social structures and species. Maybe this was the case with Pete. We were mostly the same size, so maybe land dwelling protectors didn't all need to be Royce's size. I rested my head on my knees, and Royce came to sit next to me on the sleeping platform.

We sat quietly for a time, then Royce made a throat noise and touched my shoulder. "I know this is a lot for you. Let me show you the shower, then we'll figure out what to do next."

It was awkward as Royce showed me how to turn on another switch in the small box, which made water come out over my head. He took the wand from the holder on the wall to show me what it did, then pointed to bottles attached to the wall.

"Soap, shampoo, and conditioner."

"Why?" The names were odd enough, but I certainly didn't understand why one would need three different potions for this shower ritual.

"Uh, soap is to clean your skin. Shampoo does the same for your hair, then conditioner is also for your hair so it doesn't tangle up or become too dry."

"Surface dwellers have a lot of potions."

"Right. This crap probably seems silly to you."

I laughed. "It is, but I know my skin is different out of the water. My hair too." I held out my matted hair. It smelled, which I wasn't used to. In the water, it was regal, perfect, and I missed it. Royce looked concerned.

I reached for his arm. "It is okay, Royce. I chose this."

He stilled under my touch, but his heart beat faster. I dared the one thing I wasn't sure I should do. I leaned forward and pressed my lips to his, and he froze. When his gaze met mine, his eyes were wide and searching. I was afraid I'd done something wrong, but then he reached for my face and kissed me in return.

I pressed myself to him, and he wrapped me in his large, muscular arms. My desire drove me to have my skin pressed to his, but our coverings were in the way. I was frantic to pull the shirt over my head. Royce noticed and helped. When we kissed again, my chest was against his bare skin, warm from the sun. My back was pressed to the water room door. I wrapped my legs around him and Royce responded by sliding his arm under my buttocks to hold me up. Royce's facial hair tickled and burned my new pink skin by turns with each press of our lips. I wanted more, so much more.

"Hey Royce, do you know where the pastry box..." Pete stood at the open door to Royce's room, and we turned to look at him. "Right, um, never mind. I'll be on dick. I mean deck. Fuck. I'll be up top." Pete was sunset red. He left as quickly as he'd appeared.

Royce groaned into my shoulder. "I ate them all," I said. Royce looked at me, slightly confused. "The breads in the box. I ate them all, Royce." I felt horrible that I might have caused an issue between Royce and his first mate.

Royce returned his head to my shoulder, and I felt him shake as he pressed a kiss into my skin, then put me down. I heard him laugh and watched as it vibrated his whole person. The laugh did things to my belly I couldn't quite understand, but I knew I liked it.

"Are you okay, Royce?"

"Yeah. I'm alright. It's alright." He tried to calm himself as he took deep breaths. He reminded me of a beached porpoise, the way he gasped for air.

He got himself under control enough to clear his throat and took another deep breath. "Um, let me tell Pete what happened to the pastries while you take a shower." Before I could say anything else, he left the room. I stood there feeling foolish. I shouldn't have kissed him and I shouldn't be here. But I didn't know where else to go. I hoped Royce would forgive me for my brashness. Maybe I could repay his kindness one day or become a protector myself so we could be friends and work together.

I stripped out of my coverings and stepped into the water room. I did as Royce had shown me. The water did not sting, and the liquids helped wash the salt from my skin and hair. I combed my hair with my fingers and felt the strands loosen to their more natural state. My arousal dissipated, thankfully, so I would not embarrass Royce again.

When I stepped out of the water room, I grabbed the coverings Royce left for me. I quickly put them on as Royce had shown me and sat on the sleeping platform. I could wait for Royce to return. The last thing I wanted to do was to cause him more hardship with his first mate.

BRAIDS

ROYCE

I was having a small freak-out. There really wasn't any other way to explain it. Troller had kissed me. I'd kissed him back, and it was amazing, but I felt guilty about it too. There's so much for him to learn, and I shouldn't have taken advantage of the moment. I should have stopped him, but by the sea I had wanted to kiss him ever since he rescued me. The whole thing was a dream come true until Pete showed up. I got myself under control and walked out onto the deck where Pete was organizing gear.

"Um, sorry about that," I offered as an apology. As captain of the boat, I should set an example. I wasn't doing very well at the moment.

"What do you have to be sorry for? I was the one that interrupted," Pete replied. The tone of his voice sounded off. I'd expect him to joke about it.

I glanced down at my feet, then at Pete. He hadn't stopped what he was doing. He was tense, and I wasn't sure why. "Is there something else I should apologize for? You seem upset."

He stopped moving. "No, damn it, you shouldn't have to apologize. It's your boat. You should be able to kiss whoever you want on your boat. Because it's your boat."

"Okay." I watched as he became more frustrated. "It seems like we've established that, Pete. What do you . . ." Before I could finish my sentence, Pete grabbed my face and kissed me. I wasn't sure what to do with that either. It didn't give me the same feeling as Troller's kiss. I held still and eventually Pete let go.

"Okay, so um, that . . ." Pete grasped for words.

"Didn't work."

"No."

"How long have you wanted to do that?"

"Years." Pete nodded. "Since I was a deckhand."

"What about Marcy?"

"Oh, don't get me wrong, I love Marcy. I'm going to marry her. But you and me, we worked together, so I didn't act on things because I liked our friendship. And that was probably a good thing, considering."

"So what changed?"

"I wanted to make sure, you know? Because, you and um, your merman. Wow, Royce. That was um . . ."

"Hot?"

"Surface of the sun, my friend," Pete said with a smirk on his face that made me wonder if it was envy.

"Yeah?"

"Yeah."

"Are we alright?" I watched the tension ease out of his shoulders. I held out my hand, and he took it, then I pulled him into a hug. "You're my best friend, Pete. No matter what."

"I know," he said as he patted my back. "Go take care of your guy. I've got the boat."

"Okay." I let him go. "Sorry about the pastries, it seems Troller ate them." I shrugged and Pete finally, finally laughed. It was a start, at least.

"You owe me dinner, then. Bring back some hoagies or something." Pete gave me his usual lopsided smile, and I smiled back.

"Sure thing." I left Pete with the gear and went back to my room to find Troller dressed and finger-combing his wet hair. "Can I help you with that?" I pointed at his hair.

"Yes, please, if you could? What will you do?" Troller was sitting with his legs to the side again. I wondered if that was a habit or more comfortable for him. The kiss he gave me earlier was in clear juxtaposition with his current shyness and the deceptively demure posture.

"Hair is like rope. I can braid it." I grabbed my brush and a leather binding I found on my desk. "Here, I'll show you." I settled myself behind Troller and began smoothing his hair with the brush. With Pete's kiss still fresh on my lips, I felt a little guilty.

It occurred to me that Troller was probably about a forty-five or fifty kilos less than me, maybe a little more. Maybe the same as Pete, give or take five kilos. He had a tone body with well-defined muscles, likely from swimming. While Pete was tan, Troller was pale. Pete was a good-looking guy, with short brown hair and hazel eyes. Troller was good looking as well, but built for swimming, with his broad shoulders and narrow waist. Most folks could probably tell that he wasn't human, even if the black eyes and long blood red hair didn't give it away.

Troller made soft, pleased noises with each stroke of the brush. It was utterly amusing and made my stomach do flips with each musical sound. I separated his long red hair into three parts, then handed him my brush.

"Brush," Troller stated. "Is it magical? It felt magical."

I smiled while I braided his hair. "No, it's not magical. But I'm glad you liked it."

"I did." Troller tried to glance at what I was doing, and I gently pushed his head forward again, but I caught his smile before it disappeared. "You are weaving my hair." He sounded a little surprised.

"I suppose, though we call it braiding when it's hair." I finished the last twists and added the binding to hold it together. "There. That should make it easier to manage."

He stood, and I took him in. He wore another band shirt that clung to his well-defined chest. The button-up jeans did nothing to hide the tone of his legs nor the power of his thighs. He'd also put on a pair of sandals I'd found. His braided hair hung over his right shoulder. I couldn't take my eyes off him.

"Did you need to shower, Royce?" The question broke my blatant staring. I felt heat creep up my neck from being caught.

"Ah, yeah. I should." I cleared my throat in a very failed effort to hide my frustration and the erection growing more evident the longer Troller stood there.

Troller nodded. "I'll wait for you outside."

I nodded and watched him leave, admiring how the jeans framed his ass, and barely muffled the groan I made. The shower, a quick jerk-off, and a change of clothes took me less than twenty minutes. As I stepped onto the deck, Pete and Troller were speaking quietly and the sun was shining on them. I had worried about them getting along, but that seemed misplaced. If this was a dream, I didn't want it to end.

OUT & ABOUT

Troller

Royce's face was flush when he came from his room. I apologized, as best I could, to Pete about the breads. He accepted and said Royce planned on bringing something back for dinner to make up for it. It seemed Royce was already protecting me from my mistakes. I needed to do better.

"Are you ready to go?" Royce asked. He approached but didn't touch me. Pete walked past us and gave a nod to Royce.

We were a half a fin apart. I could smell the potions I washed with earlier on him. His hair was still damp, and his covering clung to his chest. I wanted to touch him but dared not to for fear I would upset Pete. "Yes."

Royce looked behind me, and I turned to see Pete reach into his covering. He pulled out a ring of small devices. "Here," he said as he tossed it to Royce. "I fueled the vehicle. It's parked in the usual spot."

"Thanks Pete. Be back soon."

I watched as Royce stepped off the boat onto the swaying bridge with practiced ease. The narrow walkway swayed more than the boat. I wasn't so sure I could keep my footing. Sensing my hesitation, he offered his hand, and I took it. I had a hold of it for less than a breath before I stumbled. His hand shifted to wrap around my arm, up to my elbow, steadying me. "I won't let you fall."

We smiled at each other as he guided me down the bridge to the dock. I felt more accomplished about my land walking until we moved forward and my foot covering snagged on a board. Royce caught me again. My previous accomplishment melted into embarrassment, but he wouldn't have it. He put his arm around my waist and kept us moving.

"It's okay. You can lean on me until you feel more steady."

"Thank you, Royce." I put my arm around his back, and he held onto me as we walked. I nearly fell and tripped two more times before we reached a part of the land that didn't sway. The stillness of it jarred me. I pulled at Royce's arm to make him stop.

"It's better if we keep moving. You stop for too long, and you'll get dizzy. Take some breaths. It will be better once we're in the vehicle. The vibrations will help."

"How did you know?" I looked up at him, and the world swam. I turned my head back to the ground and tried not to lose everything in my stomach.

"Happens when I've been on the boat for a while. The stillness seems strange. Like being set adrift with no way to move. It passes, but you have to focus. Can you straighten up?"

"I think so," I said, as I slowly stood. Royce held me as we moved again, and I breathed through the oddness of a motionless ocean. The last time I was on land, I'd confronted Halic on a beach, and it wasn't for very long. If I planned on staying with Royce, I would need to learn how to swim in this new ocean.

When we reached the large contraption he called a vehicle, Royce opened one side of it for me. I sat in the chair, and he closed the hatch, then went to the other side, opened his hatch, and sat behind the controls. Once the vehicle came to life with a soft vibration, I understood what Royce meant. The vibrations settled me as he used the controls to maneuver the vehicle away from the dock, following markers along the ground.

"Is this a boat designed for land?" I played with the controls in front of me. Some of them responded; others did not. Blasts of air hit me, sounds blared, the glass next to me moved. Royce calmly shut things off with his controls.

"It is," Royce said as he glanced at me and looked out of the glass in front of us. "Have you seen a vehicle before?"

"I have, but I did not know what it was. Vehicles do not look like they would float very well."

Royce laughed. "You're right. Most of them can't."

"Where are we going?" I was curious because Royce had said we should do several things, none of which made much sense to me except obtaining more food for Pete.

"Well, you need clothes, so we'll go to the recycled threads store and see if we can't find you some things. Then we need supplies for the boat. And we need to find something for dinner, whether we make it or bring something back for Pete."

"Okay. You have places where you trade things for coverings, I mean clothes? I have nothing to trade, Royce."

"Don't worry, I have money. Maybe when you're ready, we can find you some work."

"Will I be assigned work?"

"No, I mean, they hire you based on your qualifications. I already have a business, and my boat is my job, my work. Everyone chooses what they want to do."

"What if I do not have any . . . what are qualifications?"

"Skills. Qualifications are skills. Like fishing or making food."

"Oh." This did not encourage me. I did not have skills that were suited for land and did not know how I would barter. Royce continued to help, and that warmed my heart, but also made my throat tight. My elders taught us to contribute to the community. So far, I had contributed nothing in the time I'd been out of the water.

"We'll figure it out, Troller. Besides, you haven't said how long you are staying."

How long was I going to play surface dweller? I clearly did not have enough skills or abilities to blend in, nor could I care for myself. "It is a good question, Royce."

"Is there a reason why you came?"

"Yes. I am not sure how to tell it." Royce said nothing. "I am not sure I can go back."

"Did you do something wrong?"

"No, and yes. They will think it is wrong. I am not the only one, but if I went back, no one would believe me."

Royce's face bunched with concern. I didn't want to worry him. My pod didn't know where I was, so we should be safe, but I wasn't entirely sure of that either.

"Are you a merfolk?"

"What is a merfolk?"

Royce pressed a button on the shelf in front of him, then took out a small device from his pocket. It looked similar to the tablet

I was using to learn his language. He spoke to the device. "Look up an image of a merfolk." He watched the device and then handed it to me with a picture. It indeed showed one of my kind, though it looked very old.

"Yes. That is what I look like in the water. Though I do not know this name, merfolk."

"What do you call yourselves?" I clicked out an answer. He smiled and shook his head. "Is there an English version?"

"Those that live in the waters that bring life is the direct translation. We also call ourselves waterfolk." It included all the species in the waters, not just my kind. Royce had asked if I was a dolphin shifter when we first met. We were not the same, but dolphins were cousins of ours.

The compartment of the land boat was quiet for a moment as I handed Royce his device and he put it away. He glanced at me and our gazes met. "You can stay as long as you want, Troller. Okay?"

I nodded, unsure of what I should explain to Royce. It would sound strange, and he might change his mind about helping me. I didn't want to lose his respect.

The vehicle came to a stop, and we got out. I watched how Royce opened his hatch and let myself out while I used the side of the vehicle to reach the hard ground—the sidewalk—where Royce met me and took my hand. I felt the tightness in my chest subside at the simple gesture.

The place we went to was small but colorful. Royce opened the door, let me walk through first, then took my hand again and led me further inside. He asked for help at the counter and a lovely surface dweller showed us around. I picked out a colorful sweater, a few more shirts, a couple pairs of half pants, two pairs of full pants, and several items that were longer than shirts but had more style to them. Royce called them dresses.

One was blue and had a reflective material that looked like scales. Royce called those sequins. As I tried it on, I imagined what it would look like underwater, and what Royce would think when he saw me in it for the first time. The thought made my skin tingle. As much as he wanted to see it, I wouldn't let him. I would save the sequin one for something special.

I noticed Royce had different feet coverings than mine. Ones that hid his toes. "Royce. Feet coverings." He glanced at his feet, then mine, and nodded. The conversation between him and the nice surface dweller was quick. I heard the word 'shoe' and connected that with what Royce was wearing on his feet.

The surface dweller came back and handed me several pairs. Ones with laces that held in place a long piece of flexible material pressed to the bottom of my feet. Ones that slipped on and off easily, like the ones I wore. Then a pair of sturdy ones like the kind on Royce's feet.

When we went to barter for the items, Royce added a package of tiny pants to the pile.

"What are those?"

Royce opened his mouth, then closed it, then said a word I had heard before but hadn't entirely understood. "Underwear."

"Do I need them?" I wasn't wearing any now, and the ones he picked out were rather plain.

"Sometimes." He blushed, and I felt my cheeks heat. If he wanted me to wear them, I would.

The nice surface dweller put everything in a woven sack, and Royce grabbed the handles. "Let's put this in the vehicle, and we can go across the street to get supplies."

"Okay."

DEAD THINGS

ROYCE

Things were going alright so far. Troller had clothes and shoes for when he was on the boat. He had picked out a few things that surprised me. He took a liking to dresses, obviously admiring the flowing skirts and loose fit. While I liked the T-shirt and jeans he wore now, it pleased me to see how comfortable he was in clothing he picked for himself. With those purchases deposited in the storage compartment of my vehicle, we walked across the street to the small grocery store.

Inside the store, I grabbed a cart and showed him how to hold on to it. As we walked, he used the cart to help steady himself, letting go of me. Losing his touch left me feeling odd, as if my spirit was heavier without him.

"There is so much green. What is this?"

"Broccoli."

"What is this one, Royce?" He held up a bunch of green stalks.

"Asparagus." He kept pointing at things, and I named them. Lettuce. Celery. Onions. Tomatoes.

"These are pretty, and they smell pretty. What is it?"

"A green apple," I explained with a smile. "They're tart. The red ones are sweeter."

"Can we have some?"

"Sure." Half the produce department was in the cart before we moved to the next section. We moved on and came to the meat department. Troller was less enthusiastic.

"What is all this, Royce?"

"Meat."

"Why does it smell dead?"

"Because it is. And I suppose that's true even for the synthetic and replicated stuff, too."

"Why do surface dwellers eat dead things?" He looked at the different items in the case and then stopped in one section. "Is this fish?"

"Yes, mostly. The genuine stuff is here, then replicated, then synthetic."

"Where are the heads? Why are they all gutted and dead?"

"Not everyone can fish. People buy things prepared for them and then take them home. Like the fruits and vegetables we picked out. It was on a vine, in the ground, or growing out of it before it came here."

"But those," he pointed to our cart, "do not smell dead. This does."

"We don't have to get any meat if you don't want it."

"I eat meat, but usually it moves. Not dead."

"I'm guessing you don't cook your food either?"

"Mostly we eat things we catch or find." The differences didn't seem like much until he pointed them out. His delight, or, in this case, disgust, amused me. Who would have thought I'd have to explain food preparation, but then again, I never expected to show someone how to use showers and toilets.

I thought about how best to bridge the gap. Maybe we could have sushi for dinner one night. Or pasta. The soup had been a hit. Maybe sticking with simple things would be better. "Okay. Maybe we stick to fruits and veggies for now. Then later I can show you how we fish from the boat." He nodded, and I smiled, fascinated by him as he took in his surroundings.

"Royce!" I turned away from the meat department to see Troller in front of the bakery. He pressed his nose to the donut case. I tried to wipe the grin off my face, but I wasn't fast enough.

"It is breads! Many kinds. Should we get more for Pete? I ate all of Pete's breads. We should have more for him." His excitement was contagious.

I walked over to him as he looked at each kind of pastry in the case with a sense of awe and reverence I'd only ever seen on a kid's face when they had chocolate or candy. "I wouldn't worry about Pete. He's seeing Marcy. She owns the bakery and makes the pastries she gives to Pete."

Troller looked at me with an intensity that made me take a step back. "How does he do that? What does he trade for pastries? Does Pete have a skill that Marcy needs?"

I closed my eyes and winced. How was I going to explain relationships to Troller? We'd kissed earlier, so maybe he'd understand. "Pete and Marcy . . . um, do you remember what we did in my cabin before Pete came in?"

"I remember. We kissed. I wanted to thank you for your help, and you liked it. You kissed me back." I could tell he was thinking about it. "Is that the skill Pete uses to barter for pastries?"

"Not exactly. Marcy gives Pete pastries because she likes him."

"So it's not barter; it's intimate."

"Yes. very."

"Ah." He paused in front of some croissants. "Do we need to get our own pastries, then?"

I grabbed the croissants. "Sometimes. Though Pete's nice and likes to share. So, if you're nice to him, he might share with you. But you shouldn't eat all of them next time."

"Right. Because Pete worked very hard and did intimate things for the pastries," Troller said, with all the sincerity of someone who had become very serious about bread in the last two days.

I covered my face, which was hot from blushing, embarrassment, and the effort it took to keep my hysterical laughter at bay. If Pete knew Troller would sell him out for baked goods, he'd be amused, then probably agree with him. It was Marcy's baked goods that had Pete after her in the first place.

"Are you okay Royce?"

His concern sent a pang of protectiveness through me. The last thing I wanted him to do was worry. I wiped my face and tried to clear my throat. "Fine," I croaked.

"You sound like a frog. Are you sure?" He touched my arm, and I patted his hand.

"Yeah, I'm fine. Really. Is there anything else you want?" He grabbed some apple fritters and put them in the cart. I picked up some eggs and shelf-stable milk on the way to pay for everything. Troller walked next to me as I carried our crate of goods back to the vehicle. The shopping trip had sparked more questions.

"I learned numbers, and those seemed like a lot of numbers for food. Does food always cost that many numbers?" His fingers played with the end of his braid. I almost tripped watching him instead of where I was going.

"Sometimes." I put the food in the rear compartment with everything else and shut the lid. "Sometimes I can trade for things during the season if we have extra, or we don't catch enough to sell in bulk."

"Not kisses?"

That comment stopped me for a moment. "Well, no, not kisses. I mean, I don't, anyway. There are others that trade things like that. Because they want to, or for money, but I haven't. Not that there's anything wrong with it if you do." I leaned on the vehicle, curious why he was asking so much about kissing. Was he worried about our kiss earlier?

"Why not? You are a very skilled kisser, Royce. Have you never found someone to trade kisses with?"

I laughed a little, thinking about what Pete did earlier and some people I dated when I was younger. I'd not dated anyone in a while and hadn't been out with anyone except my crew. "Um, no, not for a long time. Though I'm glad you think I'm a good kisser."

The setting sun caught the red of Troller's hair as he moved closer to me. "Can I kiss you?" Troller asked. I nodded, and he leaned in and planted his lips on mine. I wrapped an arm around his waist to hold him. It was soft and perfect. Nothing like the wild, half-frenzied kiss from earlier. "Thank you, Royce, for bartering for me," he said afterward.

I pulled back a little. "You're welcome, Troller, but you didn't have to kiss me for that. I would help you regardless."

Troller smiled. "I know. It's only the first of many I want to give you. I plan on earning your pastries, Royce."

I stood there, a little stunned, as Troller walked back to the front of the vehicle and got into the passenger side. I realized very quickly that I wanted Troller to have whatever he wanted. So I pulled out my phone and called a pizza delivery place. If I was lucky, it would show up by the time we got back to the boat.

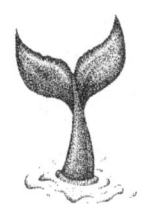

Anticipation

Troller

I couldn't tell if Royce was navigating faster than last time or if he was eager. I had been serious about wanting him. It hurt to find out that he'd been alone all this time. I had been alone, but it was because I was looking for him.

When I looked at Royce, though, it was all worth it. I'd give up swimming forever to be with him, if he asked me to.

Royce stopped the vehicle once we returned to the dock. We got out and took everything from the storage compartment. I carried my clothes while Royce carried the food. Once on deck, my body recognized the gentle sway from the gangway and adjusted to it. Then I noticed Pete in a deck chair with a drink in his hand.

"Hi, Troller. How was the trip into town?" Before I could answer, Royce came aboard, switched all the bags to one hand, fished the ring of devices out of his pocket and tossed them to Pete.

"Here are the keys. Pizza is on the way. Don't come inside for a while. Understood?"

"Aye, Captain." Pete grinned at Royce, then at me.

I went down to Royce's room. Once there, I realized Royce hadn't followed me. I turned around to head to the galley to help with the food when he appeared in the doorway.

"Were you leaving?"

"No, I was looking for you."

"Oh, good. So was I." Royce gently moved me through the doorway and closed the door. I took a step back as Royce wrapped his arms around me so his hands gripped under my thighs, lifting me. I wrapped my legs around his waist. "Can I kiss you?" Our lips were nearly touching.

"Yes," I whispered. It was everything I had wanted since we'd kissed earlier. His tongue darted into my mouth as we tasted each other. I didn't fear hurting him with my now-blunted teeth and kissed him with the same fervor. My braid swung against my back as he carried us to his sleeping platform.

We stopped kissing for a moment to remove our shirts. He had so many large muscles. My fingers traced the curves and dips of his chest as his lips traced my chin and neck. When I reached for his belt and the opening to his pants, he didn't stop me.

Royce pulled back a little to help me take his long pants and his tiny pants off. When he stepped out of them, I admired with my eyes everything I had felt pressed against me earlier. I tried to reach for his sex, but he grabbed my hands.

"Wait," Royce breathed. "Let me help you."

I'd completely forgotten my clothing. Royce removed my coverings with tender, torturous slowness. The look on his face told me he was intent on the moment. I bit my lip and kept my hands from helping him. When he lowered my pants past my hips, my hard flesh sprung up, eager for his attention.

His hand wrapped around the base of me, and a sigh escaped my throat as my hands landed on Royce's wide shoulders, then drifted to his hair. I closed my eyes, enjoying the sensation until I felt a soft wetness wrap around my sex. I looked and realized Royce's mouth was around the tip, and then he engulfed me further as he pressed my sex organ into the back of his throat. The sensations were amped tenfold.

"Oh, Royce," I said in a whisper, barely able to think. This was new to me. Or well, to this skin. This activity had never felt this warm or stimulating before.

He took his mouth away and continued the previous motion with his hand. "Is this alright?"

"Yes. It's alright," I whined softly. "Can you, please . . . more Royce." I had barely said his name when he replaced his hand with his mouth again. I held on to him as each pass of his tongue or the movement of his head continued to heighten everything I felt until I couldn't hold back. "Royce, oh please. Royce. I'm feeling—Royce!"

I pushed his head away at the last moment and watched as I splattered his chest and chin hair with my seed. He looked surprised, then I saw his gaze shift to something hungry. He opened a drawer under my legs and removed a packet and a bottle. I wasn't sure what either of them were for, but I watched as he poured a liquid onto his fingers.

He kissed me as he pressed me back onto the bed, and a moment later, I felt the cool liquid on his fingers slide into the crease of my ass. With each kiss, his fingers explored what was apparently a very sensitive place. His digits expertly caressed a part I did not know existed for my bipedal body.

"OH!" Royce froze and stopped kissing me.

"Did I hurt you? Do you want me to stop?" He was breathing hard, and his mating organ brushed against my ass.

"No, no. It surprised me. That's all." I sat up and gave him a kiss to reassure him. "It was good. Very good. Please. More."

He moved his fingers again once I laid down. I half-moaned, then yelled.

"Are you sure?" he whispered. I could hear the hesitation and concern in his voice.

"Yes! Royce. Please. Don't stop," I whimpered as I burned from the pleasure. If he stopped, I'd never reach the fire that waited on the other side, the same one he'd given me before. I was afraid that it would fall back into the embers he'd stoked. "Please, Royce. Please. I am good."

I grasped at the arm he had between my legs and pushed myself onto his fingers. I groaned and did it again. It was enough to encourage him to continue.

After he built a steady rhythm and I was on the verge of ecstasy, he pulled his fingers from my body. There was an emptiness for a moment as Royce did something with the tiny packet. Then he pressed the round tip of his mating organ into the place he had previously touched. I felt the subtle difference now and realized it must be a barrier. I wondered why Royce thought he needed a barrier, but didn't have time to think about it much as he slowly pressed into me.

The action bowed my back and had me scrambling. I didn't know which way to go. The pleasure and the burn were so intense. This was what I needed, what I wanted. The embers felt like they were being stoked to a high flame. A volcano of need welled up in me.

Royce withdrew from me, then moved onto the bed and repositioned us. I wrapped my legs around him again as he lifted my hips and grasped my ass. He slid deeper into me than before and I gasped like a fish on land. His bulk pressed me into the bed. I kissed him and held as much of him as I could while he settled into my body again, his need evident.

"Royce, don't stop. You can have this." He moaned softly as his hips moved more quickly, and our flesh made light slapping noises. I remembered what I thought the first night I saw him, floating in the water. I sang him the tones and clicks since I didn't know the words in his language yet. *"Soul of my soul, you are seen. We are one."*

I let myself crest through the wave of ecstasy. A few moments later, he cried out above me and I held him as he shook. Then I held him longer as he keened in silence as water leaked from his eyes and knew for certain what he only began to understand: We belonged together.

CONUNDRUM

ROYCE

One minute I had come harder than I'd ever had in my life. The next, I was crying on the shoulder of a man I barely knew. I felt so much and understood so little about how I had arrived at this place, with this individual I felt so much for in such a short time.

When I slid free from Troller's body, I laid next to him. The space was barely big enough for both of us, but we clung to each other. He was so very tender with me after I had been so rough with him. His fingertips brushed along my hair, wiping the sweat from my brow.

"Are you alright?" I whispered.

He nodded, and I could see his lips curve in the dim light that came in through the port window.

"Your need was great." He kissed my lips, and I gasped. I didn't know if I was going to make love to him again or cry. It was so confusing.

"I suppose so," I sighed, then laughed a little and brushed tears from my face. I wasn't embarrassed exactly, though I wasn't sure what to do with this rawness. There was one question I needed an answer to before I let myself sink further into this idea, this hope, that I had found myself with suddenly. "Will you stay?"

Troller was silent for a long time. I worried I asked a question he couldn't or didn't want to answer. Maybe I shouldn't have asked at all. There was a kind of magic in not knowing, but I had to know. I couldn't spend every day he was here wondering if this would be the last day he would stay with me. Not after everything I went through with my family. And yet, I felt selfish asking.

"You don't have to answer," I blurted. "I don't need to know. You can stay as long as you want." I sounded like a shore-side spouse. Afraid for him to leave, and afraid that if he stayed, he'd resent me for it.

Troller only smiled and touched my face. "It's very simple. If you ask me to give up the sea, I will stay with you, Royce."

I pushed him back and sat up. "What do you mean?" My instincts rang with alarm.

Troller answered me in a serious tone. "This I will do for you. It is why I sought you out, Royce. You can take the sea from me. I will let you."

"That doesn't make any sense. Why would I want to take the sea from you? It's part of who you are. It's part . . ." Part of why I fell for him the first time I saw him, but it seemed silly to say that. Especially now.

"That's not all I am. I saved you, and now you can save me."

"Are you talking about magic?" First, I had to know if it was permanent. Second, I needed to understand for sure what Troller was asking.

Troller looked confused by the word magic, but I didn't know how to explain it. "I would become like you. I would stay. You can do this."

"No, I can't. I don't have magic." Why did he believe I had magic?

"You do. All surface dwellers have it."

"Not all of us." I was perplexed. I'd never done a magical thing in my life.

He touched my chest, his hand over my heart. "You do, Royce. I can feel it. You can take the sea from me."

"No," I said in disbelief. "No!" I said more firmly as I got out of bed. I retreated to the bathroom to clean myself off and flushed the protection I'd used. The agitation I felt only grew as I found my underwear and put them on. "I would never take the sea from you. It's part of who you are. Why would you want to give that up?"

Troller sat naked on my bed as I paced the small space between us. "You want me to stay with you, yes?" he asked.

"Yes! But I don't want to trap you here. I don't want you to resent me." I turned circles in the small space. "By the sea, I envy you. You can go places I can't and move with such grace." I took his hands in mine and knelt in front of him, catching his gaze. "I envy your life and the freedom of it. You don't need things. You can live in the present and not have to worry about food or shelter. Why would you want to leave that?"

Troller cut me off before I could keep going. "You. Know. Nothing. My life is not what you think, Royce."

I shook my head. "What do you mean? I don't understand." He pushed me away, then stood and pulled on his pants. As he opened the door and left my cabin, I felt a sudden panic until I realized he went down the hall instead of toward the deck and the water he'd wanted me to take from him only a moment ago.

When I found him, he was in the box of apple fritters. I watched as he picked out a pastry and took a huge bite. With his prize in hand, he sat at the small galley table, and I sat on the opposite side so I didn't block him in.

"I'm sorry, Troller." If Pete heard us or saw me in my underwear, I didn't care. I was more concerned about the man in front of me eating his way through a box of pastries.

"I don't have the right words to explain. It's not your fault, Royce. I asked for too much, too soon." He took another bite, and my heart hurt to watch him look that way, distant and fearful. I'd done that to him. But if I'd understood him, I had some ability to take part of him away. I wanted so much to understand, and two days wasn't nearly long enough. I watched as he took a deep breath and let it out. "It's alright Royce," Troller said. "Maybe I was wrong. Maybe you can't take my other form from me."

"Maybe." I found some sticky spot on the table I had missed cleaning earlier when we'd eaten sandwiches. I licked my thumb and tried to clean it off, focusing on that spot instead of his words. His words broke my heart. The sea saved me. He had saved me. It made me wonder what had happened to him, that he didn't feel safe there. The more I thought about it, the more alike it seemed we were. I had only found safety here, on my boat, sailing the sea. "If you stay for a while and decide you never want to return to the sea, I'll help you."

We were quiet for a long time as Troller ate. I attempted to lighten the mood between us. "I want you to make sure I'm worth all the breads first before you give up something you can't get back," I said.

Troller's smile was worth everything to me as he took another bite, then offered a piece to me. I took a bite and realized I was hungry, too. "Is there another in there?"

He laughed and handed me one, saying, "I remembered not to eat everything I haven't earned yet." I took the pastry from his hand and met him halfway with a kiss. It would be alright. I had to believe that because the last thing I wanted to do was lose him. We didn't talk about the sea or magic. Later, we returned to my room and explored more of each other.

CLARITY

Troller

The days turned into weeks, and I learned everything I could from Royce about his boat, what he did, how he interacted with the sea and his love for it.

I understood now why he had refused my request. For him, it would have been worse than death to lose something so important. For me, it was a chance at a new life. I had to make him understand. He still refused to believe he had any kind of magic, but I could sense it every time I was near him. All surface dwellers had it. I sensed it from all of them. I couldn't figure out why they continued to deny it.

Pete and Marcy were lovely, and once Marcy knew how much I loved the pastries she made, she sent extra with Pete. In return, Pete, Royce, and I spent a lot of time doing chores and bigger maintenance projects in Marcy's shop.

Royce and I spent time reconfiguring the captain's cabin to fit both of us. Regardless of whether I stayed with him, at least he'd have a space that suited his size. It baffled me how he had squeezed onto his platform, then somehow he made room for me as well.

"When will the parts for the foldaway arrive?" I asked.

"Next day or so. We can remove the platform bed and shelves today so the space is ready. The new one can go against the wall where the desk is now and we can move the desk and storage to the wall opposite the bathroom. We'll have space when the bed is up, but not much when it's extended."

We got to work removing the shelving. In one drawer, I found a picture of a family. The adults in the picture were wearing similar clothes. The child was looking up at his parents, a proud look on his face.

"Royce, is this you? Are these your parents? What do the clothes mean?" I held up the picture.

"Fuck," he mumbled. "Yes. Those are my parents." He pulled the picture from my hand and put it back in the drawer, then took the drawer from me and walked out of the cabin. "We have a lot of work to do."

I stared at his back as he walked out. "Royce," I called after him. "Royce!" I wondered why he didn't have the picture displayed somewhere. It was customary for surface dwellers to display photos. I'd seen them often enough in the empty vessels in the depths of the sea.

He had found something to do in the in the captain's nest. I slowly approached to not startle him. "What's wrong, Royce?" He tensed as I touched his back. I removed my hand, but stayed in his presence. "Are they no longer living?" It was the only thing I could think of that might upset him.

"No, they're fine. My parents are retired and live in Florida."

"Can we visit them?"

"If I try to visit them, then the world follows me. They know that."

"What do you mean?"

"My parents." He took out the picture. "Their clothes are military. My father, Leopold, but everyone calls him Leo—he's a prince. My other father, Ben, was part of his guard until they fell in love. The whole thing caused a bit of a stir, but since Leo was the third son, he cut ties with his family, though the press still followed them. They sent me to boarding school when I was ten. I'd only come home when necessary and after I graduated college, I rarely visited to keep the media from swarming us."

"Royce, that's so sad." He sighed and I reached for his free hand to comfort him.

"My parents wanted me to have a normal life, and they knew if they came anywhere near me, the media would follow." He took a breath. "The minute someone recognizes me, everyone swoops in like vultures, looking for the 'lost prince.' The only place I've avoided the madness is on the sea. We've stayed in touch and talk a few times a week."

"Royce?" He looked up from the box. My gaze met his.

"Yeah?"

"Do they have a boat?"

"They live in Florida. Everyone there has a boat."

I looked around at what we were standing in, and I watched the idea form in his head. So I pushed a little more. "I want to meet them. First, we should finish fixing the cabin. After that, maybe you could suggest that they could meet us somewhere in the Gulf."

"Yeah." He smiled. "I think that would work. I mean, we can try it at least."

He stood and wrapped an arm around me, then gave me a kiss. We talked about dinner before he left me and went to the deck with his phone. I returned to his room and continued cleaning out the cabin.

Humans collect so many things. I found fishing hooks, loose bits of wire, charts that were out of date, and other items that I piled up for Royce so he could tell me what he wanted to keep or recycle. When he came back to the cabin, he was still smiling.

"We're meeting next week! I'll see if we can borrow Pete's cruiser. It's small but more maneuverable." Royce's excitement was infectious.

It made me wonder. "Does Pete know about you and who you are?"

Royce shook his head. "I didn't want to put that on him."

"He's your best friend Royce, tell him. He knows about me. What could it hurt if he knew about you as well?"

He walked toward me, and I straightened as he wrapped his arms around me again. "How did I get so lucky to have such a smart partner?" The word "partner" warmed my heart. Royce finally understood what I already knew. We belonged together.

"I'm not that smart. Just . . ." in love, I thought, though I kept the words in my throat. It was too soon for him to accept them. "I want you to be happy. I don't want to be in the way of that. Ever." That earned me another kiss.

"You'll never be in the way, Troller."

We continued working. At some point, we stopped for food and sex against the wall. When we finally called it a night, we piled bedding on the floor to rest. With Royce curled at my back, deep asleep, and his arm lightly draped over my waist, I tried to sleep, but my thoughts were restless.

The port had been a haven. If we went into open water, the pod could find me. There weren't that many pods in the Gulf, but we communicated with others that inhabited the area, like dolphins and whales. If my pod caught me, they would take me back to punish me. Halic would make sure of it.

As if Royce instinctively knew what I was thinking, he pulled me toward him. The heat from his body was like the sun warming a rock. I wanted to stay near that warmth for the rest of my life.

OH FOR PETE'S SAKE

Royce

I left a message for Pete to stop by in the morning. He still worked for me, but spent less time on the boat since we were between seasons. I hoped we could work out the details of where we were going and explain why. Troller was right. My friend deserved that.

Pete stuck his head into the galley, where Troller and I were having coffee.

"This is surprisingly more dressed than I expected either of you to be this morning. Did someone die?"

"No, no one died. That's odd. Why would you say that, Pete?" Troller asked.

"Okay, now I'm more worried. Him," Pete pointed at Troller, "he doesn't get sarcasm, so his response makes sense. But you," he turned back toward me, "why are you so quiet?"

"Come sit with us. Please."

Pete put a box of pastries on the table and sat down. I took another drink of my coffee while Troller opened the box and pulled out a fritter.

"We're going to Florida next week. I wanted to let you know so you could deal with anything that comes up while I was away. Plus, we were hoping we could borrow your boat."

"You don't want me to go with you?"

"I'll be with Troller. We'll be fine."

"No offense, but Troller barely knows anything about boats. What if something happens?" Pete tensed. I hadn't meant to slight him and thought he'd be more than happy to have a week with Marcy.

"Troller knows the seas. We'll be fine, Pete."

"But what if..."

"Pete."

"What?"

"We're going to meet my parents." Pete's eyes widened.

"Then don't you think it would be better if I were there?"

"No. For one, they don't enjoy meeting new people that much, and for the other, they don't like being recognized."

Pete was quiet. I narrowed my eyes at him and realized he hadn't asked the obvious question after that. "You know."

Pete nodded.

"How long have you known?"

Pete stood, then paced the galley. It was like watching one of those Rube Goldberg machines go through twists and drops. Something seemed to click, and he abruptly sat and looked between Troller and me.

"I knew this day would come sometime." Pete shook his head. "Um, Royce, your parents hired me."

I was too stunned to talk, but he continued.

"They wanted to make sure you had someone with you that could protect you if something happened. I never expected that the boat would be the thing that might take you. When you fell into the drink that night, I should have been on deck with you. I thought I killed you. All this time we've been friends, and I wanted to tell you—"

I didn't realize what I'd done until Pete was against the opposite galley wall with a bloody nose. "You lied to me?" I felt like someone had stabbed me in the guts with a fishing spear. "You've been on my boat for ten years, Pete. I trusted you."

Troller moved, and I didn't stop him. When he came back with an ice pack for Pete's face, I felt myself clench my fists. "Why are you helping that asshole?"

"I'm helping him because when you calm down, you'll realize you've hurt your friend more than he's hurt you," Troller said.

I got up from the table and headed toward the hatchway. Pete wheezed as he spoke. "Royce, they were worried about you. I wasn't the first person they hired to watch you. I quit five years ago."

"Why did you stay?" I looked over my shoulder.

"Because you're my friend, asshole. Isn't that enough?" Pete said. I walked out of the galley and headed to the deck to think.

At that moment, I questioned everything. I thought I'd earned this boat from the previous captain. Worked on it, paid my way and worked up from deckhand at twenty-two to first mate by the time I was twenty-five. Pete showed up a year later, looking for a job. He had recently finished a tour in the International Navy and was used to more sophisticated boats, but he caught on fast enough. I never considered that my parents had been involved.

Ten years was a long time to stick around. Fifteen years on the same boat was a good run, wasn't it? At thirty-seven, I could take my savings and go somewhere else. Sell the boat and disappear to an island. Troller could come with me. It sounded perfect in my head.

I felt a hand on my back. "How are you feeling?"

"Upset." I turned and wrapped Troller in my arms. "We've been friends this whole time, and he said anything. Then a month ago, out of the blue, he kissed me, and—"

Troller tried to push out of my arms, and I tightened them to keep him in place. "Let me go, Royce. I'm going to punch him myself."

"It wasn't like that Troller, it was harmless, and before anything really happened between us." Troller looked like he wasn't sure it was harmless. "I promise." He sighed, and I pulled him closer. "I was surprised, that's all. I thought we knew everything about each other."

"You thought he didn't know about you being a prince," he offered.

"Fuck." I sighed again. "Yeah, you're right. But he did. I only wish he'd said something."

"Like, I'm sorry?" We turned to look at Pete as he stepped onto the deck with a bit of cloth pressed against his nose. "Listen, I am sorry. I wanted to tell you, but eventually it didn't matter anymore. You seemed like you needed a friend more than anything else, and I didn't see the point of bringing up shit you didn't want to talk about."

I sighed. "Pete. I forgive you. And I'm sorry for popping you in the nose." I tried to stay mad, but I didn't have it in me. Troller was right. All he'd ever done was try to protect me. Well, except for the kiss, but that turned out to be nothing. "Now, get off my boat."

"Aye, Captain." He walked toward the gangway.

I called out, "Tell Marcy I'm sorry that she has to deal with the likes of you for an entire week."

"This number you did on my nose is going to garner me a shit ton of sympathy, and you'll be in the doghouse when you get back. Oh, and you can borrow my boat. I'll give the marina a call so you can pick up the spare key fob from them."

"Thanks, Pete."

Pete waved as he walked down the dock. "Later, Royce!"

I pulled Troller in close and leaned against him for support. Guilt over bloodying Pete's nose made my stomach churn. In the grand scheme of things, his friendship meant more to me than whether we knew each other's secrets. Pete had stayed and built a business—a life—alongside mine. That told me our friendship meant more to him, too.

THE GULF

TROLLER

Royce had the coordinates for where to meet his parents. I was excited about meeting them and wondered what his fathers would be like. The whole month we'd been together, Royce hadn't asked me much about where I'd come from. He kept his questions within my personal sphere, and I appreciated that.

Royce introduced me to some new things. I liked bread and soup. Pasta was my favorite. I loved just about any vegetable or fruit Royce found, and I loved Royce. Eventually, I'd have to explain why I was here, and why I stayed with him instead of returning to the sea. We were so focused on the present that I didn't want to spoil it with the past.

We dropped anchor about a third of the way to our destination. It would take two more days and one fuel stop before we would reach our desired location. Royce was doing a last check for the night when I felt an urge.

"We should go for a swim." I stripped off my sundress and tossed it to the side. Royce watched, looking distracted, then shook his head.

"I don't think it's a good idea."

"No one's out here and it's a pleasant night. We won't go far from the boat. Besides, I'm not taking no for an answer." I went to the aft of the boat, stepped onto the small dive deck, and jumped.

"Troller!" I saw Royce from under the water. My body wanted to shift, but I was holding it off. "Troller, answer me."

I surfaced near the boat. "I'm here. Are you going to get in, or will you make me come back up there and pull you in?"

Royce gave me a look and shook his head. He quickly stripped, then jumped into the water. He came back to the surface spitting.

I swam toward him. The smile on his lips was playful, then his eyes narrowed. "You haven't changed."

"I was waiting until you were in the water. I didn't want to scare you."

"I'll close my eyes if you don't want me to watch."

"You can watch." I dove under the water and shifted. It took a few minutes, though it felt like forever. When I came back up, I cleared my gills and blinked at Royce.

"You look exactly like I remember. Well, except your hair wasn't braided." His smile shifted a little. His lips thinned but barely kept from being a frown. "I don't remember the teeth. Those look sharp."

I grinned at him and he flinched, splashing water, then laughed. "It's a good thing I know you or I'd be pissing myself right now."

Royce tread water until I wrapped my arms around him and swam for both of us. I gave him a soft kiss with a small trilling noise of excitement. It was nice to be near him in my natural form.

"Can you talk? Or is it different?" he asked.

I pointed at my throat and my gills that I had to dip into the water to breathe. Royce nodded.

"Right." He brushed his fingers along my face. I felt his fingertips trace my ear and cheek. It reminded me of what I'd done when I first met him. "The scars on your neck and torso make sense now. Those were your gills, sealed up?" he asked. I vocalized my agreement with his observation. "I'll take that as a yes?" I nodded.

"You're absolutely stunning."

I gave him another smile with a soft trill, and he laughed.

"Maybe you could teach me to understand you in this form?"

I nodded. It was possible, but I didn't think Royce could ever make the correct noises with his human throat. We held each other a little longer, and while I wasn't cold, I noticed Royce shiver as the sun set completely.

I swam us to the ladder and urged him to go up first. He didn't protest, and I observed as he used his powerful arms and legs to haul himself out of the water. I had watched him the night he went overboard. His determination and stamina were nearly unmatched, even by waterfolk standards. Even without my help, I believe he would have survived. His strength and size were attractive to me and made me feel safe.

I held onto the ladder as I shifted. The cold crept along my newly formed skin as my scales floated away on the eddies that swirled around me. When I had feet again, I climbed the ladder. Royce was there with a towel he wrapped around me the moment I stepped on deck. I reached for him. Royce held me while he dried us off, then wrapped the towels around us as we stood together, admiring the stars.

"Was that the first time you've shifted back since you've been with me?"

I nodded. "Ports are tricky. Lots of places to hide, but also a lot of places I can't. I didn't want to risk it."

"Does it hurt to be out of the water for long periods of time?"

"It hasn't been a problem so far." According to Halic and the council, going to the surface meant a painful death. To drown on land, gasping for breath. I know differently now.

I lifted my head from his chest and looked up at him, then pressed my hand to his face. My fingers slid along his beard and dropped to his chest.

"Do you want to tell me more about home or where you come from?"

It was an innocent question, but I tensed in his arms. He noticed and held me tighter, his voice dropping to a whisper in my ear.

"It was enough for me to know that you wanted to be with me, Troller. I didn't ask because I didn't want to explain my own circumstances. You can tell me when you're ready."

Royce continued to prove his kindness and caring. I thought about not telling him, but he deserved an answer. I took a breath and explained what my life was like before I arrived on his boat.

"We're warned to stay away from the surface." There was a slight chuckle from Royce, but I tapped his chest and he quieted. I felt his fingers play along the plait in my hair.

"The surface always fascinated me. I watched other waterfolk have the freedom to venture close and even play with others, but my species kept our distance. There were stories from a long time ago about how we were hunted for magic. There was a time when we could shift, leave the water, and walk on land. We were told it was no longer possible. We'd die if we tried."

"Is that why you thought I had magic? That I could change you with it?" Royce asked.

I nodded. "We were told it was possible. That surface dwellers had magic that would make us like them. And I would never have to go back."

"Then you'd lose everything you were. You'd always be in your bipedal form. You'd never be able to see your pod again."

I nodded.

"The one that spoke of it the most lied to us. An elder of ours named Halic was secretly going to the surface. He has abilities none of us have which gave him power over the council and our people. Everyone fears him." Royce held me tighter, and I clung to him as I continued talking.

"One day I followed him. I watched from a rock outcropping as he pulled himself up onto the shore and shifted. He said words I didn't understand and went into a building that wasn't there before. Once he went inside, I swam to shore and discovered I could change as well. I was so weak the first time. After I practiced and watched a few times, I grew bold."

"Royce." I choked on the words in my throat. The sorrow I wanted to express seemed too large for it. "I confronted him. For me, for my pod. I asked him why he said such things if it was possible that we could all walk on land again? He knew I was right and spoke words I didn't understand. I think the words forced me to shift while I was out of the water. If not for a large wave that swept me out to sea, he would have killed me.

"He's part of the council that governs us because of his magic. If I went back, it would be my word against his. I would have been banished, or worse."

Royce held me close, pressing me into his chest as I keened softly. I hadn't realized how much I had held in by not talking about why I left everything I'd known.

"Then, it wasn't luck that you were in the water that day."

I shook my head.

"You were following Halic?"

I nodded. "He almost caught me when I saved you. The whistle you heard was Halic calling the pod. It brings us to him. Either it wasn't as effective above the water, or something about you let me resist it long enough to avoid suspicion."

Royce looked at me with his light brown eyes. "After the accident, I dreamed about you and how you touched my face. You seemed curious and scared at the same time. I kept hoping you'd come back. There was a moment that I thought about leaving the boat for good, but I didn't, because I hoped you'd find me again."

I smiled at him. "It worked."

"Yeah, I guess it did."

"I was curious about you, too. There were a lot of places to look. The only thing I had was the name of your boat. I'm a fast swimmer, but I'm not as fast as a boat. I didn't know where or what Galveston was, either." Royce kissed the top of my head. That small reassurance was everything.

That time before I saw Royce again had been frustrating. I didn't know where I was going, nor did I have the means to search away from the water. I had to find caves during bad weather, avoiding other pods and waterfolk that might betray me.

"Now that you've found me, we'll figure out whatever comes next together," Royce said.

"Yes, together is good." I gave him a squeeze around his waist.

He gave me another kiss on my brow. "I'm starving. Let's make dinner," Royce said, then he slapped my ass. I was not proud of the noise I made.

"Can we have pasta?" I asked.

"We had pasta yesterday. What about tacos?" he asked.

"I guess." I shrugged as Royce laughed. I loved his laugh and would do anything to continue to hear it for the rest of my days.

COASTAL WATERS

ROYCE

The water was calm as we arrived at the coordinates my parents specified. There was only one other boat in the area. I'd never been on it, but I'd seen pictures. The *Guardian* was floating serenely in all its massive glory. It made Pete's boat, *First Draft*, look like a river raft. I pulled the cruiser next to the yacht and Troller threw the fenders over the side. We gently bumped into the *Guardian* as Ben and Leo worked with Troller to secure the boats.

Leo, Ben, and Troller were introducing themselves across the gap as I powered down the cruiser. Both my parents stopped and smiled at me as I went to the starboard side of the tiny aft deck.

I had Ben's black hair and tan looks. He often said it was a family trait. I also had more of his build, though I was larger than him. He also had light blue eyes and an engaging personality that got on my nerves sometimes but charmed Leo to no end.

From Leo, I had my disposition, a quiet demeanor, and light brown eyes, but not his red-brown hair or freckled skin.

When I put a hand on Troller's shoulder, he looked back at me and smiled. My parents caught it, and Leo gave me a knowing smile. There would be questions, but that wouldn't be until someone poured the wine.

Troller and I transferred to the *Guardian*, and I should have known that Leo would have a perfectly catered meal ready for us. All they had to do was heat it. They had come alone, with Ben driving the boat while Leo navigated.

"This was a great idea, Royce. I don't know why we didn't think of it before. We should have," Leo said.

"It was Troller's idea. He wanted to meet you both," I said. I took a bite of the bacon wrapped asparagus appetizers, which were my favorite.

"How did the two of you meet, anyway?" Ben asked as he poured wine for everyone.

"Ben." Leo shook his head. "Too soon," he whispered.

"Honestly, it's a bit of a long story. It might take most of the evening to explain it," I said. Ben shot Leo a smile and sat down. Leo brought over a tray of lasagna, and I knew Troller would be in heaven from the first bite. Once our plates were full, Troller and I explained how we first met and who Troller was between bites.

"Are you serious? You're a merman?" Leo asked.

"That's not what we call ourselves, but yes," Troller said.

"I need more wine." Ben smiled and poured himself another glass. "I heard stories growing up on the coast around the isles, but no one ever had proof."

"A lot of our pods swam with the boats or were on them when they came to these lands. What stories we have still mention the crossing."

"So why reveal yourself to Royce?" Leo asked.

"I had my reasons," Troller said. He shot me a smile, and it warmed my heart. Leo looked between Troller and me and smiled.

"Then it took nearly a year before he found me again. We've been together for about six weeks," I said, then took a drink of my wine.

"I'm happy for you, son," Ben said. "No offense to Troller, but we're a little surprised. Where's Pete?"

"You mean the Pete you secretly hired to spy-slash-protect me? That Pete?" I tried to keep my tone playful, but the stunt annoyed me. I should have expected it. It was like them to interfere and be overly protective.

"I told you that wasn't a good idea," Leo said to Ben.

I got the sudden impression that maybe Ben had picked Pete for other reasons besides protection. That was pretty typical of him, always thinking five steps ahead. I always wondered how much attention Ben paid to details like that. My parents would have received reports from the school, and bodyguards would take me to and from the place. I felt like I knew my guards more than my parents sometimes. Though I had to admit, for Ben to have found someone like Pete meant he had paid attention to me in his own way.

If Pete and I had any kind of chemistry, he would have had something to crow about for years. Half the reason I had a boat in the middle of the ocean was so I could live my life how I wanted. For Ben's sake, I'm glad it didn't work. Who knows what that would have done to our relationship?

"He's dating a lovely woman named Marcy. She owns a coffee shop close to the port in Galveston," I explained, as I broke the awkward silence.

"She makes wonderful pastries. Pete thinks so too," Troller said in a suggestive tone, and Ben almost did a spit take. It was good to laugh with my parents. I hadn't seen them face-to-face in a long time. They were older, but still healthy and doing well. I felt young again and happy, eating dinner with them without an audience.

As the night went on, I noticed how easily the conversation flowed between Troller and my parents. We talked about our trip out, the weather, my plans for the next season, and Troller's ambition to be a deckhand. Troller ate his third helping of lasagna, and we had a lemon custard for dessert. It reminded me of the nights when we didn't have social duties and my parents would send the staff home so we could have dinner as a family. It happened less and less as I grew older. The time was slowly taken away by more formal dinners and events.

I hadn't resented the time we spent entertaining people. I knew about the work my fathers did for the royal family. Even though they were retired, it was important. They organized charities, projects, and general concerns that covered everything from multi-specie healthcare to space missions. They expected me to learn the whole routine and follow them one day. The fishing boat hadn't been part of their plan, but it grew on them. I wondered how much of that was Pete's doing, rather than our weekly conversations.

Ben poured himself and Troller another glass of wine and offered to show him around the Guardian while Leo and I cleaned up. After we had everything put away, he poured us both a single finger of whiskey.

"He seems nice. Is everything going alright?" Leo asked.

"Yes, Papa, everything is going pretty well, actually. We're happy." At that moment, Leo did something I hadn't expected. He opened his arms and pulled me into a hug.

"I'm so very happy for you, son." He gave me a squeeze and let go as he thumbed tears away from his eyes. I pulled him in for another hug.

"Don't cry. Pop will rearrange my face if he thinks I made you cry." I patted Leo on the back and let him lean against me.

"No, he won't. Not if he knows what's good for him." He finished his drink, and I finished mine.

I laughed. "I'm going to pretend I didn't hear that. It's something for the two of you to figure out."

"What do we need to figure out? Royce? Leo?" Ben asked, and I saw Troller behind him with a smile on his face. Ben caught sight of Leo's face and shot me a look. "You didn't make your Papa cry, did you?"

"Pop, he did it all on his own. Promise." There was some soft laughter as things settled down.

"I showed Troller where the two of you can sleep if you'd like. It's bigger than the cabin on the cruiser, so you can stretch out. In the morning, I can make everyone a proper breakfast, then later we can go for a swim." Ben walked over to Leo and looped an arm around his waist.

Troller's eyes pleaded with me, and I couldn't say no. I nodded to Ben. "Alright, sounds good."

Leo clapped his hands together. "Perfect!" He grabbed another bottle of wine and motioned for us to follow. "Let's sit out on the deck for a while and catch up some more."

My parents talked about sports and various charities they were involved in. We talked about the remodel we had just finished on the *Aire Apparent* for the captain's cabin and some of the work we did at Marcy's shop. After we finished the bottle, all of us sat in silence, watching the water and the stars. Ben finally called it a night as Leo dozed on his shoulder. Pop helped maneuver Papa into a standing position, then they wandered off to bed. Troller and I stayed on the back deck a little longer.

"Your parents are nice." He leaned his head on my shoulder, and I wrapped my arm around his to bring him closer.

"They aren't bad people. They aren't even stuck up. I sometimes wonder what it might be like if they could have been an average couple with a kid."

"How so?"

"When their relationship became public, Leo being gay wasn't the issue, not even for the royal family. Things had advanced enough that having a genetically related child with a same-sex partner was commonplace." I played with Troller's hair as I talked. I rarely had to explain who my parents were; people knew. It was one more thing I appreciated about Troller. I had time to tell their story before someone made up their mind.

"What stirred the pot was the fact that Ben was Leo's primary guard. Ben's former lovers were all too happy to talk about his failed relationships with the press. When Ben was summarily dismissed from service, even though Leo had taken the blame, Leo left his life as a royal to be with Ben. While Leo's family was upset, Ben's family was livid." Troller caressed my chest as I spoke. It calmed me.

"Ben is from a family of elite guards that have a long history of protecting royal families. They are rumored to have a power that can take down dragons, but dragons have not attacked royal families in centuries, so who knows? As for the royal family, Ben being pansexual wasn't the issue either. It was that he broke protocol so badly with Leo that he tarnished both institutions. Or so they thought, which is why his family disowned him. Really, all it did was resurrect their organization from the ashes. Having a Saint George Knight as a bodyguard came back into fashion, and anyone with clout, fame, or royal lineage clamored to hire any capable member of the family if only to project the idea that they might be swept off their feet by some dashing icon of bygone days."

"Did Ben's family ever change their mind or apologize to him?" Troller's voice was full of concern.

"No, they didn't. But when they married a year later and had me, the royal family was a bit more accepting. They were invited back, but Leo turned them down and offered the current arrangement of charity work and the occasional royal function instead."

Troller nodded. "With all the challenges you and your parents had to deal with, I'm not surprised you've kept to yourself for so long, my love."

I lifted an eyebrow at his statement. "My love?"

"Yes?"

I laughed. "You're drunk."

"So? Why does that matter?"

"It doesn't. But we'll see if you call me that in the morning." I grinned at him.

"My love, I'll call you that whenever I please. Unless you really don't like it." Troller got up from his side of the bench and settled on my lap, facing me. His sun dress slid up, exposing his thighs, distracting me for a moment before I met his gaze.

"I never said I didn't like it." I touched his face, tracing the curve of his cheek. "I like it a lot, actually. My love."

He leaned down and gave me a kiss, and I couldn't help but kiss him back. We were pretty heavy into a make-out session when someone made a noise behind us. Ben stood there frozen as he realized we had caught him watching, then turned to the cooling unit and pulled out a water bottle.

"For your Papa." Ben grinned, then turned back toward the main suite. "Carry on."

When Ben was out of sight, Troller and I laughed softly.

"Should we go to bed?"

"Probably."

"Should we sleep in Pete's cruiser?"

"Nah. This tub has more soundproofing than that cabin. Which reminds me, we should look for a sound dampening spell before the season starts. We don't need the entire crew hearing us."

"Aye, Captain."

"Now that was hot." I lifted Troller into my arms, stood, and carried him back to the other suite on the starboard side of the *Guardian*. I was ready to find out what other words I could entice out of him.

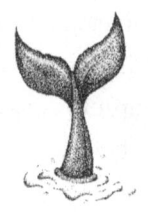

LIKE ROYALTY

Troller

Royce's parents were wonderful. Lasagna was my new favorite food besides pastries, and we had more space than either of us knew what to do with. While I was excited to spend time with Royce's parents, I somewhat missed our clean but sparse room back on Royce's boat.

Royce stopped kissing me long enough to call out a voice command. "Cabin, dim the lights seventy percent."

The lights dimmed, and I was in awe. "Is everything voice-activated?"

"Not everything. There's a panel on the wall too. It seemed too bright, and I didn't want to put you down long enough to mess with the controls."

He put me on the bed and pressed against me. His lips were warm and slick from our kissing, and his beard rasped in the most delightful ways. I wanted more of his skin against mine.

"Fast or slow?" he asked.

"Fast. Fast, Royce. Please! I need you."

"Don't worry, love. I need you too."

Maybe the wine was doing more of the talking than I wanted to admit, but the need to be naked with him was overwhelming. Clothes came off, and Royce lifted me easily and adjusted our position on the bed.

When his hardness brushed mine, I pressed my hips up for more, and Royce pressed himself down onto me. His mouth devoured mine as he found a quick rhythm. As the frenzy cooled a little, he pulled back, then sat back on his heels and looked around. I was half in his lap with my knees on either side of him, our cocks gently touching each other with the sway of the boat.

"There." I pointed to a drawer. He reached over and opened it, took out the bottle, and thankfully didn't ask. I had looked while Ben had taken me on a tour of the boat. I wasn't surprised to find, like Royce, the men that owned this boat made sure it was well stocked with supplies.

Royce opened the bottle and poured what he needed into his hand. He took one large hand and pulled me further up his lap while he wrapped his other large, lube-covered hand around both of us and began a slower pace that made me squirm and moan. I thrust my cock into his hand and used his body for leverage where I could.

"Royce," I breathed. "That feels so good, my love."

He went faster, and I covered my face with my arm as I panted. I could feel myself on that delicious drop-off, waiting for the deep water of pleasure to engulf me. Instead, Royce rolled us. I hadn't realized I was being moved until his hand left me and an arm scooped me off the bed.

Royce looked up at me, and I looked down at him, heart beating fast, face hot from my near-orgasm. He reached for the lube again and poured more on his hand. When his lube hand reached for my crease and then slipped a finger between my cheeks to tap at my hole, I clawed at his chest, grasping hair. Royce gasped in response.

He slowly slid one of his thick fingers into me, and I rocked back on it, pressing it in further. I reached between us and clasped our stiff spires, and worked them over the best I could. I wasn't quite able to wrap my hand around us both the way Royce could, but I still made him moan with my efforts.

When he pressed a second finger into me, I slowed my hand. I wanted him inside me. I wanted us to come together. The burning warmth he created felt so good, and I knew Royce would feel that much better. I pressed back a little more, rotating my hips to work his fingers in deeper.

"Royce, please," I begged.

Royce nodded and pulled out his fingers. He dumped more lube in his hand, took hold of himself, lifted my ass, and set me perfectly on the crown of his cock. I never failed to be impressed with his strength and deftness, especially while we had sex.

I wiggled my way onto his shaft, slowly sliding down until there wasn't any more to take. We sat there for a moment, reveling in the feeling. When his hands gripped my ass cheeks and moved me with a slow lift, I didn't try to hurry. Everything tingled. The lights in the room seemed to dance like the stars outside. My whole body was drawn tight, waiting, needing exactly what Royce gave me with each thrust.

He moved me a little faster, and I reached for my dick. I stroked myself at the pace Royce set. Needy moans left my lips as he drew out then pressed his entire length back in. I enjoyed the fullness of him and the space he left behind. A reminder of him until he returned.

On his next thrust, he angled himself to push at that sensitive spot he'd found in me, making me cry out with pleasure. I was in awe of the leverage he had from his prone position with my weight on top of him.

"Again, my love. Please. I'm so close, Royce." I leaned down to kiss him, and he nearly slipped out of me. When I leaned back, he pressed in, just so far, and pulled back out. He made small, quick thrusts into me, right over that spongy flesh that never failed to drive me wild with need. I felt my genitals tighten and throb in my hand. A few more thrusts and I spilled my seed onto Royce's chest.

"Fuck, Troller, you feel so good," he grunted and pushed into me completely, which caused me to spurt again, and then Royce swell inside of me. He thrust hard and fast as I rode him.

"Yes, my love, that's it. Give me your seed," I panted.

"Fuck, Troller, fuck," he cried as he groaned with one last thrust and came. His hands squeezed my hips to stop me from moving, but I pressed myself down onto him and clenched my hole around him. He cried out again and I squeezed harder. "Mercy, please. Mercy," he panted, then chuckled as I let up. We smiled at each other as we caught our breath.

When he finally softened, I leaned forward and let him slip out. The product of our lovemaking cooled on our skins, pressed between us. I rested my face on Royce's chest as he wrapped his large, muscled arms around me, and let out a relaxed sigh.

"We should clean up," I suggested.

"Sure. One more minute," Royce said.

He groaned as I rolled off him. "Look, the shower is big enough for both of us. Or at least it looks that way. Help me clean up?" He seemed to come to life at that offer. I held out my hand, and he took it as he levered himself out of bed.

Royce was in awe of the shower. He kept playing with the settings. Eventually, we cleaned each other off with these small towels that Royce called washcloths. Before we were through, Royce removed the braid from my hair and washed it.

"I could spend the rest of my life helping you take care of your hair." He meant it, and I wanted that and more.

"Where did you learn to weave hair, Royce?"

"The guy that owned the boat before me made sure every hand on his boat could make knots, sew, weave a basket, and braid just about anything. He wouldn't promote anyone without it. Since I wanted to be a captain some day, I learned more than I needed to so I could impress him."

"Did you have a relationship with him?" I asked, wondering if this previous captain had broken Royce's heart.

"No, not like our relationship. He was my mentor and understood what having a life of my own would mean to me."

Royce rinsed one potion from my hair, then applied another and continued talking about his mentor.

"He taught me how to do the job, then was good enough to let me figure out how to make it my own. For instance, I'm not as strict. My folks need to know knots and basic sewing. Anything else is extra."

While he rinsed the second potion from my hair, I turned to kiss him. It was gentle at first, then evolved into an exchange of hands, helping each other to another orgasm.

When we slipped back into bed, clean and satisfied, Royce pulled me close and kissed my forehead. Right as we were about to drift off to sleep, he whispered, as if someone might overhear him.

"How do . . . ? When you were in your other form, I noticed you didn't have um . . ." He paused.

"A penis?"

"Yeah."

I laughed and buried my head in his chest.

"What?! I'm curious."

"Uh huh," I said in a mild tone that meant I knew there was more than curiosity. "We have pouches. It keeps our genitals safe and eases swimming. You wouldn't want to swim very far with your genitals hanging out."

Royce laughed. "I can imagine."

"There are different ways to engage in intercourse under water." I could see Royce's eyes widen as I kissed him. "I'll show you tomorrow."

"Promise?" He wiggled his eyebrows.

"Promise." I kissed him and sighed contentedly. "Cabin lights off."

As the room shifted into darkness, we pressed closer. I couldn't imagine a more perfect day, and tomorrow would be even better.

Anatomy Lesson

Royce

My parents shared looks while Leo cooked breakfast in the spacious galley the following day. Pancakes were his specialty, and Troller was in heaven again.

I leaned over to whisper to him. "You know, if bread was a person, I'd be jealous."

"Lucky for me, it's not," he whispered back, then turned to my parents. "Leo, these are divine. Does Royce know how to make these?"

"I taught him when he was a boy, you remember, Royce?" Leo gave me a big smile as he flipped another pancake.

"I remember. I also remember exploding blueberries and Pop coming into the room thinking someone had shot us."

"Oh bloody hell, I remember that," Ben laughed. "That was such a frightful mess to clean up."

I explained to Troller, "The blueberries were frozen. We weren't sure what happened, but we put a bunch in one pancake, and it sprayed batter and blueberry bits all over us. Pop came into the kitchen to find Papa and me standing next to the stove, completely covered. He nearly freaked until Papa stopped him and explained what happened."

"That sounds traumatic. I'm surprised you still like pancakes," Troller said.

"I do, but not ones with blueberries." I laughed a little, and everyone was grinning. We had replicated bacon, eggs, fruit, cheese, and more. There was enough food to last us through until lunch, which was probably the plan.

Sometime later, we all changed and jumped into the water to enjoy the nice weather. Troller almost didn't wear trunks until I explained that while they might not care, Leo and Ben were my parents, and I didn't want to embarrass them if they did.

Troller acquiesced, and we spent the morning doing races along the length of the *Guardian*. While I and my hundred-thirty-six kilos gave Ben a run for his money, it was Leo and Troller that were more evenly matched in size and musculature. Regardless, Troller easily beat us all, even in his bipedal form.

Eventually, Leo, Ben, and I ended up on the swimming deck watching Troller dive and surface repeatedly. By mid-afternoon, Troller swam to me and put his head in my lap, his legs trailing in the water, while my parents and I were drinking beer and enjoying the sun.

I smoothed back his red hair and played with his braid. He looked at my parents, then me. I caught on pretty quick. "Do you want to change?"

Troller looked up and nodded. I looked over at my parents. "Would it freak you out if Troller changed?" I hoped it wouldn't. I wanted Troller to be comfortable.

"There's a lot of fish. I could catch dinner," Troller offered.

"No need for that. We have plenty of food. And you're our guest, Troller," Leo said. "Please, feel free to be yourself." Leo smiled, but it didn't reach his eyes. If anyone understood, it would be him and Ben.

Ben nodded. "Come on, Leo, let's grab a few more beers so Troller has some privacy."

I smiled then, and so did Troller. He quickly stripped out of his trunks and handed them to me. When my parents came back and took a seat on the swim deck, Troller surfaced again.

They put down their beers and looked between us. "Hi, Troller," Leo said. "Are you more comfortable?"

The high, pleased trill Troller gave in response had us all laughing. I explained. "His vocal cords are different with gills, so he makes vocalizations in this form."

Troller acknowledged what I'd said with what seemed like an affirmative whistle.

"That's pretty amazing," Ben said as he put his hand on Leo's knee. "You both seem happy. I know I've said that before, but seeing you together makes your father and me happy, too. We were worried about you for a while."

"I know." I watched as Troller dove under the water. "It's the first time that I feel like it means something. No one's ever made me feel like this before. No one's ever meant more to me than him. Well, except you two." I turned to look at them, and they had soft eyes. "Don't you two start crying, dammit. You old softies." That did it, and we were all laughing through our happy tears. It was tough on all of us while I was growing up. They dealt with a lot and stayed next to each other through it all. Supporting each other even when the world seemed set against them. If they could do it, Troller and I had a chance. We'd come from different places, different worlds even, and because of that, we loved our differences and each other.

Troller was gone for a bit, but I could tell he had something in his hands when he came back. He swam to my parents and motioned for them to hold out their palms. When they did, Troller placed a pearl in each one. The pearls weren't perfect, but they were big.

"Did you find oysters?" I asked.

He nodded and grinned. He swam over to me, picked my mask and snorkel off the swim deck, and tossed it to me. I looked at my parents. "Apparently, we're going oyster diving." They laughed as I jumped back into the water.

"Thank you, Troller," Leo said. "These are amazing!"

"Yeah, thank you," Ben said. "You two have fun. We'll see you when you get back."

I put on my mask and diving snorkel, then Troller took my hand. We dove under, and he led me along the bottom until my lungs burned for want of air. I pulled at Troller's hand. He looked back, and I pointed up. Instead of letting me grab a breath, he pulled me closer and wrapped his hands around my face. I tried not to struggle as he pulled my snorkel out of my mouth and sealed his lips over mine. He blew a breath into my mouth and I gasped with need.

I clutched him and tried to pull away at the same time. Fighting instincts wasn't fun. We hadn't done this before, and Troller hadn't warned me. He probably thought I could handle it. But once I was comfortable, it was one of the most singular thrilling experiences of my life. To breathe and be underwater with no equipment. Just Troller, breathing for me.

We went back to the surface, and I pulled my mask down around my neck. I was more enamored with Troller than ever as we floated together.

"That was amazing, Troller. I didn't know we could do that."

He nodded and gave a soft looping trill I couldn't figure out, so I gave him another kiss in response. He reached for my hand and slid it down his front until it reached his groin. It was smooth except for a perceivable bump behind what felt like a crease in the skin.

My hands weren't small, so I nearly protested when Troller took two of my fingers and pressed them into the crease. As they slid inside, I felt his hardening cock nudge my fingers. "Oh, shit. That feels interesting." Troller made a chortle with a soft moan as I slid my fingers up and down the length of him through the slit of his pouch. I felt myself respond. Troller noticed.

He caressed me through my trunks, and I groaned. When he reached inside, he avoided touching me with his claws as he took my cock out. His skin could probably handle it, but mine certainly wouldn't.

After that, it was a matter of letting Troller guide me. The closest comparison I had was probably the first time I'd had sex. I remember it all being painfully slow, even as I wanted to come so badly. My partner was more experienced, so their patience helped.

Troller brought me to him and coaxed me into wrapping my legs around him. It took a few tries, but I knew as soon as I slipped into him. We both gasped as my solid length slid up along his. It was tight, and the pressure was almost too much until Troller encouraged me to move my hips.

He leaned back in the water, and I thrust into him, my hands braced on his hips so I wouldn't float away. It was erotic and weird at the same time. Then Troller reached for my head and pulled me to him for a kiss. We quickly sank below the water. Troller breathed for me as we settled to the seafloor and fins swished to keep us in parallel. I took my hands off his hips and reached for a couple of rocks below us, then used them to push and pull myself while trying to let Troller breathe for me.

When I came, it was so fucking intense that I gasped and immediately sucked in water. Troller grabbed my head and breathed for me again. I kept going until he vibrated under me. Another burst of warmth surrounded my cock. While it felt different, I didn't want to pull out. Staying warm was always a factor, and as I shivered, Troller gently pushed me back after giving me a full breath and pointed up. I nodded. We broke the surface, and I fixed my swim trunks while I kicked to maintain my position.

"Holy shit, Troller." I swam closer and gave him another kiss. He kissed me back and made a purring noise. "That noise is new. What does that mean?"

He looked at me, reached out and traced a heart on my chest, then pressed his hand into it. I think I had a pretty good idea. "Fuck if I didn't wish I had gills. Troller, I love you too."

The purring noise was louder as we kissed again. I wondered how long we'd been away from the boats. We were far enough that I could barely see them.

"Are you alright?"

He nodded, and I grinned at him. I righted my mask and put the snorkel back in my mouth. Troller took my hand and swam us back to the boats, remembering to bring us close enough to the surface so I could use my snorkel to grab a breath.

My parents were watching sports on the holo as I got out of the water. Troller changed back while I grabbed a towel for him. We spent the rest of the day watching movies with my parents and eating whatever food they had brought.

Leo asked about the oysters, and I told him we didn't have any luck finding more.

He looked between the two of us and shrugged. "Maybe next time," Leo said.

I kissed Troller's blushing cheek and smiled. It was a good day. I wanted it to last forever.

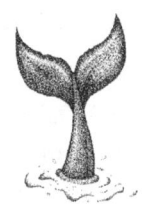

New Season

Troller

Returning to the *Aire Apparent* was like returning home in a way. I had grown fond of the space Royce and I had created. The captain's cabin was spacious and easy to keep tidy. Between when I'd arrived on Royce's boat, to when we left to visit Royce's parents, I had collected several clothing items. I even had a few more dresses in my collection.

Royce and I chatted with his parents whenever we could and made plans to spend a week somewhere on the water during our next downtime. Royce seemed lighter for it. Leo noted once that Royce was less somber and more animated now when we spoke with them.

There was still a lot of work Royce needed to do for the boat to be ready by the time the season started. Pete worked with Royce during the week and spent his weekends with Marcy.

In the meantime, I learned how the fishing gear worked and studied another land dweller language. While English was Royce's language, I discovered that Marcy and Pete spoke Spanish. Practicing with Pete and Marcy helped. Royce tried to learn too, but had problems with the "double r" sound.

One evening over dinner, we tried to practice, but only succeeded in annoying Pete, who was napping in the crew quarters next to the galley after a long day of working on the engines. It was a Friday, and normally he would have returned to Marcy's, but the maintenance had run later than expected. He mentioned something about her having to wake up "at the crack of dawn" for a special order, and he thought that showing up on her doorstep so late would be unwelcome.

"Why isn't Pete in his cabin?"

Royce shrugged. "Probably didn't want to muck it up. He was covered from head to toe in engine grease and old sea water last I checked."

"That's not fair to the crew."

"They aren't here yet. Won't be for another few weeks."

"Will he clean it before they arrive?"

Royce laughed. "Those quarters have seen more muck, grime, and body fluids than a college dorm. Pete adding to it won't hurt anything."

"Royce." He stopped with a bite of pasta halfway to his face. "How will it look if I'm staying with you, and the crew stays in filth?"

He put his fork down and looked at me. "It's not that bad. Honest. I'll show you." He got up from the table and I followed.

Pete looked like something an octopus had ejected. There were stains on the mattresses. Half the storage wasn't useful because of missing or broken bins. Not to mention the stains covering nearly every surface.

"See that stain there?" I glanced in the direction Royce was pointing and saw the brown splatter on the wall. "I made that when we were riding out a storm and my dinner came up unexpectedly. No one could do anything about it. The smell was horrid. We were confined to quarters for nearly six hours before I had the chance to clean it. By then it had dried and became one of the many permanent marks on the place."

It didn't impress me. Pete laughed. "Then there was that one time you invited the blond from the bar back to the boat since you had night watch—"

"Pete," Royce said. I glanced at Royce.

"—thought you would get a little action—" Pete continued, either ignoring the warning in Royce's tone, or not caring.

"Pete, seriously."

"—and the subtle rocking of the boat made him barf in your lap."

"Pete!" Royce yelled.

"Oh, hi Troller." I laughed as Pete rolled over in the bunk he was occupying.

"Asshole," Royce said.

"What? Troller knows you aren't Captain Innocent. And dealing with the horror that is the crew quarters is a deckhand tradition. You learn to live with it."

Royce gave me another shrug and waved in Pete's direction, as if his statement proved his point.

"Fine, I'll stay here," I said.

"What?" Royce said, surprise written on his face. Pete sat up slowly, glancing between us, suddenly interested.

"If we won't fix the crew quarters, then I'll stay with the crew." Royce opened his mouth to protest. "You've said it yourself, and so has Pete. The crew has to trust each other. As the new person, I need to earn their trust. How will the crew react if I'm staying in your newly remodeled cabin while they stay here?"

I looked around the room. It was disgusting. I felt bad for the crew I hadn't even met yet. Back home, water would have flowed through a space like this, and moss or small cleaning fish would have taken care of any large messes. I would play cleaning fish to make sure the crew had nice quarters for the season.

Pete looked between the two of us. "Not to take sides, Royce, but Troller's right. It would start the season off on the wrong foot with the crew. They wouldn't say anything to you, but they might to me or Troller. It's a good idea to head them off before they feel some kinda way about it."

Royce glanced at me, sighed, then held up his hands. "Alright. We can redo the crew quarters."

"Good. Start with Pete."

"What?" Pete's surprise amused Royce, making him laugh. "Hey! I was on your side," he said.

"And I thank you. Now you need to take yourself to your cabin, shower, then eat dinner. We'll talk about what to do next."

It didn't take long to fix up the crew quarters. A few coats of paint, new storage, mattresses made from stain resistant materials, and new privacy curtains, gave the space a brighter look, and a much better smell.

I was putting the finishing touches in place when Royce stopped in the entryway. "You were right, Troller. This looks a lot more welcoming." He was covered in grime, and clearly didn't want to track any into the newly renovated space.

"You're a mess. All done with engine maintenance?"

"Yep, all good and ready to go next week."

"Good. I'm done here too. You clean up and I'll make dinner."

"What are you making?" He tried not to have a skeptical note in his voice, but I caught it. While my language skills were exceptional, my cooking skills had not improved. My last few attempts to make dinner did not go well.

"Peanut butter and jam sandwiches, with sliced apples and more peanut butter."

Royce grinned. "Sounds good to me."

I went to him and gently kissed his lips without touching him. "Good, so go already. We have the boat to ourselves tonight. Pete already showered and left."

Royce gave me another quick kiss and headed to his cabin. I smiled, watching him as he walked down the narrow passage and disappeared into the open hatch, ducking his head slightly.

A week later, I was presented to the crew as they came aboard for the season. Pete did the introductions.

"We have a new greenhand on the boat this season. I'd like you to meet Troller. I'm assured that he is pretty handy with the gear, but don't ask him to cook dinner. For all our sakes, if he ends up on galley rotation, it'll be sandwiches and we'll all be grateful. I'll leave you all to get acquainted."

The crew chuckled. I gave a little shrug, but it was all true. Pete waved me forward, and I moved to the first in line to introduce myself.

"The name's Kristy. I've been Royce's second for a few years now. Glad to have you aboard, Troller." We shook hands, which I was much more comfortable with now that I understood the gesture. "Your braids are cute," she said with a smile as I tried not to blush.

"Thank you." Royce had helped arrange them in loops around my head to keep my hair from being caught in the gear. "I like yours too." Kristy had tight braids in a pattern along her head that were gathered into a knot at the back. Hopefully, we'd be able to chat later about hair styles. Royce's hair was too short to braid. It would be nice to practice again, and learn Kristy's style.

I moved down the line, and met Chris, who asked for my pronouns and I responded with he/him while Chris told me theirs. They had hair the color of fish scales. I discovered they had dyed their hair so it would show different gradients of color. "Did you dye yours too?"

"No, this is my natural color."

Chris smiled, but their eyes were envious. "It's amazing. Your red is so vibrant."

"Thank you." I wasn't sure what else to say. I knew it wasn't a surface dweller color. My eyes weren't either, but no one mentioned that.

The last person I met was Jamie. She was short and well-muscled. Her blond hair was braided, as well as her beard, which was the same color. We shook hands, and she smiled up at me. "Is this your first time working on a boat?"

"Yes. Though I've been around vessels my whole life." Which was true. "I used to dive around wrecks and recover things that were still useful." Which was also true and the story Royce, Pete, and I told the crew for now.

"That's brilliant. I've done a bit of remote salvage work myself. Risky stuff. Maybe we could compare wrecks sometime." She said it in such a way that I wondered if Jamie was flirting with me. It was obvious Pete thought the same thing as he interrupted the conversation.

"Okay, enough introductions. Time to stow gear and get to work. We leave dock after the last supplies are loaded. Kristy, do a final check on the traps. Chris and Jamie, bring aboard the supplies and get them stowed. Troller, follow me. You're on bait prep."

"Harsh, Pete," Chris said.

Jamie piped up as she followed Chris. "I've got a special soap you can use to take off the stink when you need it, Troller."

Chris laughed. "Stop flirting, Jamie." She shrugged as they disappeared down the gangway.

Kristy smile at me, then patted my shoulder. "Good luck, Troller. And definitely take Jamie up on that soap or your hair will smell like bait for a week," she said as she moved to check the gear.

Pete waved for me to follow. We went down another set of stairs that led to a large compartment below the living quarters and most of the forward deck. It held the tanks that would carry the fish we caught and a large prep station. I could have found it by the smell alone.

"It stinks, but when you bait the traps with it, it attracts fish for kilometers."

"Must cause some sort of chemical reaction with salt water that fish are drawn to."

Pete looked at me for a moment and shook his head. "Gotta hand it to you Troller, for someone that's only been top side for a few months, you've adapted really well."

"It was a matter of survival. Besides, I didn't want to be a burden to Royce."

He smiled. "I don't think Royce would see it like that, and frankly, neither would I. You saved his life. That's not a simple thing to forget. I could have lost a friend that day. Even though I don't know the reason, I'll be forever grateful you were there."

"Thanks, Pete." It meant a lot that Pete felt that way. I know Royce did too. Still, it was important for me to contribute. It's what they taught me to do. While my first home was lost to me, I was determined to be a caretaker for the home I found with Royce and his crew.

He nodded. "Now, let me show you how we put the bait together." We put on gloves and masks to keep most of the stink off of us. Pete showed me how to mix up the meal, then roll it in an edible gel that also stank. When we were done, we put the final ball-shaped bait into a rack in a deep freeze next to the table. When we reached our first area to set traps, my job would be to send bait balls up to the top side via a bucket system, and then replace them with new ones in the deep freeze.

It was late in the evening before I was done. When I walked into the galley where everyone was enjoying a beer, I noticed the only one not there was Royce.

Jamie took a sniff. "How in the seven realms of hell do you not smell like a rotten egg right now?"

I grinned at Jamie as I grabbed a beer for myself out of the fridge. "You don't think you're the only one that has soap, do you, Jamie?" The crew laughed. Pete hid a smile with a drink of his beer.

"Oh ho, well then, I stand corrected." She smiled. "Would you like help with your hair?"

I smiled back at her, not exactly sure if it was a friendly offer or more flirting. "Thanks, but I have that covered, too."

Pete jumped into the conversation, possibly desperate to change the subject. "Troller worked on the crew quarters. You all should thank him for the upgrades." There was a round of cheers to that.

The crew kept chatting until the boat slowed and we heard the anchors drop. Pete finished his sweet fizzy drink he called soda pop and stood just as Royce showed up at the galley hatch.

"Boat's all yours, Pete," Royce said.

Pete moved past him with a nod. "Aye, Captain. Have a good night."

"How's everyone doing?" Royce asked. There were general replies to the positive, and then he looked at me. "Do you want me to braid your hair tonight or leave it down?"

I smiled as everyone else was suddenly quiet. "You can braid it."

"Well then, let's shove off. I'm relieving Pete in the morning." I stood, and Royce offered his hand. A small shock went through the crew as I put my hand in his.

I glanced back at the table and noticed they were all looking at me. "Sorry, Jamie. Better luck next time."

Kristy snorted, then Chris joined her, followed by Jamie. Before we were halfway down the passage, there were hoots and hollers, with various sentiments of encouragement for Royce.

Once we were in his cabin and closed the door, he gave me a kiss. "How was your first day?" he asked.

"Pretty good, my love," I said as I put my arms around his neck. "Pretty good."

LEARNING CURVE

ROYCE

When we came back into port during the first break of the season, Troller and I stayed on board while everyone else ventured into town. They had a good first week, and Troller had kept up with them from day one. He joined the crew for meals and each night we went to my cabin together.

I had worried about what they thought and checked in with Pete. Troller had been right, and the remodeled crew quarters had helped along with Troller doing his best to keep up. Everyone was impressed, according to Pete. He mentioned Kristy was happy for me, too. It was a load off knowing that the crew accepted Troller. While I was satisfied that everything was going well, Troller still had concerns.

"It's obvious to your crew that I'm not human, but they don't ask what I am," Troller said as we lay in bed together.

"I'd be surprised if anyone was purely human anymore. A lot of families have branches of their family trees that are related to other species. There might even be a few distantly related waterfolk around the docks or working on boats."

"Surface dwellers no longer discriminate against others?"

"Well, I can't say that, though I wish that was the case. Some do, but mostly, everyone co-inhabits places more peacefully than they used to. And as far as the crew's concern, they likely find it interesting, but they won't ask because it's none of their business. They only care about how well you do your job and that I'm not giving you special privileges."

Troller narrowed his eyes playfully. "Isn't sleeping with the captain a special privilege?"

"Only if it disrupts the day's work." I turned toward him a little. "I can't say I haven't been tempted. Especially when you wear those blue shorts and your tank top." He laughed, and I kissed him. I loved hearing him laugh.

Since meeting my parents, we took more chances by going out for a few hours in the open water every week for him to shift and swim. Pete knew since I had him take over the boat on the nights we went out.

Often we'd pick nights that the open water was calm, with little mammalian activity. When the crew broke for dinner on a quiet Thursday night after a decent day's fishing, I saw Troller coming toward the stairs to the nest and knew what he planned to ask. I held up a hand. "I'll let Pete know we're going for a swim." Troller grinned, nodded, and went to get things ready. While it felt weird to me for Troller to ask permission to swim, he thought it was for the best. It was his way of showing respect for my position.

Our excuse to the crew was that Troller needed a few night dives to keep a certification he didn't actually have or need.

No one questioned it since we'd been able to maintain Troller's backstory about being a wreck diver. We took the boat's tender and diving gear to keep up the pretense.

As we got about a hundred meters between the boat and the shoreline, I dropped the small anchor to keep it stationary.

"Tonight, we'll practice names again," Troller said.

"Do you ever think I'll be able to say your name with this throat?"

"Not really, but you should be able to remember the tones well enough to vocalize them."

"You say that now," I laughed.

"I believe in you, my love," Troller said as he rolled off the side of the boat. He tossed his trunks back at me, and a few moments later, I was looking at Troller, the waterfolk. He propelled himself out of the water for a moment and gave me a quick kiss before he dove back in.

While I still worried that our little night adventures weren't as risk free as we thought, I also knew that if Troller didn't swim, it would be the same as if I took his other form from him. Most times, I rarely got out of the boat. Tonight I did because Troller insisted I needed to feel his chest vibrations along with his vocalizations. He'd told me that feeling the words with my body was just as important as vocalizing them.

Troller did a low to high scale of notes while he pointed to himself. I repeated, and he repeated it again. When I successfully repeated his name with my vocal cords, he got a pleased look, and I realized his name must have been simple compared to mine. Click and a vocalization, then another click. I tried learning the tones for my name, but they never came out quite right. When Troller and I got back on the boat, he laughed. "You'll get it eventually, my love. Don't be so hard on yourself."

"Easy for you to say. You have the right vocal cords." He shrugged. "Is it just me, or is shifting between the two forms becoming easier for you? You don't seem like you are in as much pain anymore."

"You're right. I've also been able to shift more quickly. It's not completely without discomfort, but it doesn't last as long." He looked thoughtful for a moment. "I imagine before waterfolk hid, we probably shifted between breaths like it was the most natural thing to do."

"Maybe someday, it will be like that again," I offered.

"Maybe." Troller looked back toward the boat while I started the engine and pulled the anchor. When I glanced at him again, he was actively scanning the water for something.

"What's wrong?" I yelled over the engine.

"I thought I saw something."

"Like what?"

"Dolphins." He shook his head. "Maybe I imagined them."

"You didn't hear anything, did you?"

"No," he said, with a frown on his face, unsure of his answer. "Maybe it was a reflection off the cove."

"Are you sure?"

"I don't know. Unlike them, we were making noise."

I reached for his hand, and he took it. "It'll be alright. If they send someone for you, we'll deal with it."

He nodded. It was clear from the look on his face that he wanted to believe me. I wanted to believe what I said too, but in truth, I wasn't sure at all.

THE BLUE DRESS

TROLLER

About halfway into the season, the crew and I surprised Royce with a birthday party. We'd come back to our port for the weekend. As we finished mooring, Marcy came down to the dock and Pete helped her aboard. They set up the cake, and I got dressed. I'd been saving my sequin dress for a special occasion, and this seemed like a suitable moment.

The crew gathered behind me as we lit the candles on the cake. When Royce yelled to find out where everyone was, we came out of the cabin area onto the deck, singing a traditional song of Royce's people to mark the occasion. I held the cake in my hands as we approached Royce. The look on his face was the best present I could have asked for. I had learned about birthdays through Pete. We didn't have such things among my people, plus we reckoned time differently under the water.

"Make a wish, Royce," Pete said as he patted his friend's back. Royce looked right at me and blew out the candles. When he took the cake from me and handed it to Marcy, I wasn't sure what was happening until he took my hand and pulled me into his arms for a kiss. The crew celebrated around us, and Pete herded the school of fish back to the galley for cake.

"What was that for?" I asked.

Royce ran his hand along the sleeve of the dress I was wearing. "It was for being you. That's what it was for," he said.

I kissed him back, and he wrapped his arms around me. "You let me be me. And that means a lot." Music came up from the galley, and we started swaying. Royce spun me around. The dress flared a little, catching the fading light as it shimmered with dark blue sequins in swirling patterns. It had beautiful shoulder slits, draped perfectly across my body, and wasn't too long, so it showed off my thighs. I couldn't understand why everyone didn't wear dresses more often. It might not be practical for working, but in my off time, they were comfortable. In the water, it would have been perfect for my other shape, too.

He touched my hair, then my face. "Is this the reason you had me braid your hair differently?" Instead of the normal braid Royce usually did for me, I had explained the way to weave my hair in smaller braids that came together like how one might make a basket out of reeds, then smaller braids to hang down my back. Jamie had mentioned to me that the style had similarities to her own. Jamie, Kristy, and I often talked about how we braided our hair.

I nodded. "On important occasions with my pod, I would have my hair woven similar to this with the addition of family tokens. It means just as much to have you braid my hair in a similar way."

Royce was quiet for a long time as we danced. "I know you miss them and if you had another choice, you wouldn't have left."

"If Halic had given me another choice." I shook my head. "I have you in my life, Royce. And that's worth everything."

We held each other until Pete found us. "Are you two going to come eat some cake before these vultures eat it all?" Pete asked.

"We'll be right there," Royce said, his voice soft but strained. His gaze met mine. "This is the best birthday I've ever had."

"It's not over yet," I said with a big grin. Royce laughed, and that sound brought so much joy to my heart, it was fit to burst.

We had cake, wine, beer, ice cream, and so much singing. It turned into an entertaining night on the boat. The crew stayed up, Pete and Marcy left for Marcy's place, and eventually Royce and I went back to our room. The soundproofing spells were proving invaluable.

It was quiet in our room as Royce kissed me, and we swayed with some shared, unheard music. When his hands slipped to my buttocks, I stopped him, though I regretted it a little.

"Wait, wait . . . I have one more present. But I wanted to give it to you when we were alone."

"Oh? Does it require getting naked? I like this present already."

I shook my head. "Sit down, and I'll get it."

He sat on our bed and watched as I pulled the gift out of one of our storage bins.

"How did I not see that? That's our underwear bin, isn't it?"

"When's the last time you retrieved your own underwear?" The storage was on my side of the bed, so I often selected our clothes for the day.

He laughed, "Okay, you have me there." He reached out and pulled me into his lap.

"I have no complaints, my love. Besides, I enjoy helping you get dressed." I handed him the box.

The box wobbled in Royce's hand and I thought for a moment he might drop it. I held my hands out to catch it. I didn't want the contents harmed.

"It's heavy," he said in a curious tone. I nodded. He reached around me to tear off the paper. It revealed a wooden box. He opened it and saw the iridescent purple liquid sealed into a bottle. When he saw the small envelope in the lid, he put the box down and took out the note.

I knew what it said. I'd helped organize it with his parents. The secret was hard to keep from Royce, though the look on his face as he read the note from them was worth it. I kissed his cheek and wrapped my arms around his neck as he cried. Leo's handwriting was distinct.

Dear Royce,

We wanted to get something for you we thought would be special. So when Troller said the crew was going to have a party for you, he helped us figure out the perfect present. This is from the three of us. It's a transfiguration potion. It will let you be like Troller for as long as you stay in the water.

It's no small thing to say we love you. Ben and I wish you and Troller a long and happy life together.

All our love,

Leo & Ben

P.S. - Follow the directions. When you break the seal, it should change color to let you know it's ready.

Royce looked at me. "I had to send them some of my cast-off skin after I shifted. Leo knew someone that could do this kind of magic. They really love you, Royce."

Royce smiled. "They love you too. They did this knowing that they might never see either of us again if I take this potion." He traced his fingers over the bottle, then put the note on top of it and closed the lid.

"Your parents want us to be happy. They want you to be happy."

"How did they even know?"

"I might have mentioned that you said something to me about wishing you had gills."

Royce laughed. "I bet Pop was not thrilled with the idea."

"On the contrary, Ben was very agreeable. To make sure we received the package, he arranged for a personal courier to bring it to me. He also arranged for a courier to pick up the ingredients when they were ready. He was worried about security and people knowing we had something like this."

"Now that sounds like Pop." Royce smiled.

"Do you like it?" I was nervous. I didn't want to push him to use it, but I wanted him to have the chance. I dared hope for something that I hadn't thought possible. I could not survive Halic on my own, but maybe with Royce, we could return home and challenge him together. Or we could start our own pod, away from the others, and teach them what I knew. As the dream formed in my mind, Royce distracted me.

"I love it. It's the best present I've ever had. You're so amazing, Troller. I'm incredibly lucky you're in my life."

Until that point, I had kept my emotions in check. I had seen Royce cry. The salty water they called tears were such strange things. Whether we were happy or sad, waterfolk made vocalizations. I made a cheerful tone that made Royce smile as he dried my face, caressing it with his thumbs, removing one salty tear after another.

"You're crying. It's okay, love," Royce whispered.

"It's your fault. You taught me." He laughed. I buried my face in the crook of his neck and eventually laughed with him. As my tears stopped, I became very aware of Royce's hands on my thigh and my back. It was his way of comforting me, but it was having another effect.

I lifted my head to look at him. His beard outlined his kissable lips, which were curved in a smile that was all for me.

"So, where were we?" Royce asked.

I took the box, stood, and put it back in the underwear bin. When I returned to Royce, I knew where his mind was, and it was far from sleep. When his hands gravitated to my buttocks again, I didn't push him away. I leaned down to kiss him as he slowly slipped the straps of my dress off my shoulders, then unzipped the back just enough to let the dress fall from my body onto the floor.

Royce stopped to admire me. "You're wearing panties." They were a blue lace that matched the dress, though they barely hid anything, thin as they were.

"Kristy helped me. She said they went with the dress. Do you like them?"

He nodded and dragged them down my hips and off my body.

When I bent to untie the laces wrapped around my calves from the sandals I wore, Royce stopped me. "Leave those."

Then he stripped out of his shirt as I pulled at the drawstring of his shorts. His hands drifted slowly up my thighs until they caressed my ass cheeks. His fingers gently spread them, and his middle finger moved to graze my hole, but found the plug instead. The smile on Royce's face widened with a hint of deviousness as he gave it a small tug. The moan that slipped out made Royce hum in a low tone. When he tried it again, I relaxed, so that the flared end would easily slide out.

"Oh wow," he said as he held up the metal plug with a small glass jewel on it. His face was full of wonder at the size and then changed to shock. "Kristy didn't help you pick this out too, did she?"

I shook my head and laughed. "The internet helped me. Kristy might have given me a website. You've been paying me wages, and I thought I could spend a little to make your special day worth it."

"You are worth everything I have, Troller. I need nothing else."

We kissed as his fingers filled the space and played with the gland that sent a zip of pleasure to my brain. When Royce couldn't stand it any longer, he removed his fingers and replaced them with his hard cock. I was ready and lubricated, which allowed me to take his entire length with his first thrust. My hard-on was pressed between us, leaking onto Royce's stomach.

"Troller, Gods above." Royce held onto my hips as I rocked on his lap. I wrapped my arms around his shoulders, kissing and nibbling his face while we coupled. When he came, I held his face in my hands and repeated the words I had said before. Except this time, they were in English.

"Soul of my soul, you are seen. We are one."

"Troller." Royce's eyes filled with tears as he kissed me. We caught our breaths as he looked at me. "You've said that to me before, haven't you? The first time we were together."

"Yes, my love." I ran my fingers across his chest, playing with his chest hair. He was so much larger than me, even if I was stronger. He made me feel safe in his arms. When I sought him out, that was all I had originally wanted, a measure of safety. But it became so much more than safety, even after the first two days. I knew I wanted to be with him for as long as he would have me. "How did you know?"

He laid back and brought me with him, so I laid on his chest. "Your voice sounded the same, even though the words were in English. Like you were repeating the lyrics to a song."

I smiled, proud. "Very astute. See, you're learning my language already."

He grinned. "Maybe I can have you sing more for me." He moved at a speed that belied his size, rolling to pin me under his body. Then he moved until his head dipped between my legs and his ass was in my face. He took my half hard cock in his mouth and I grabbed the globes of his ass in response. He moaned around my growing hard-on, which sent shivers up my spine.

Royce had pulled out our bottle of lube earlier, before he realized I had prepared for him. I seized upon it and poured some onto my fingers, then gently rubbed them between the cheeks of his ass. He immediately moved his hips as he continued to suck, and I inserted them. With a few delicate touches, I found his gland and teased it.

I bit my lip and thrust my hips up to feel more of his mouth on me. Royce rocked between my dick and my fingers, pleasuring me as he pleasured himself. "That's it, my love. Just like that. Make me sing for you." He moaned his agreement. I made tones indicating my pleasure as I spilled into his mouth. He sucked at me until I could take no more. He pressed his hands into the bed, framing my hips. I continued with my fingers, and then reached for his cock with my hand, gently working him over.

"Troller, gods, that's it. Like that. I'm going to come." He groaned and splattered us both with his seed. I watched as he heaved in great lungfuls of air, then swung himself off me, twisting to sit on his ass, his right foot near my mouth. We smiled at each other until I leaned over and licked his smallest toe. Royce's eyes shot open as he watched me lick and suck each one. When I reached his big toe, he was hard again. "I had no clue I would like that so much."

"How is it different from sucking on your fingers?"

He had a curious look on his face as he thought about it. "Technically, it's not. I guess." He smiled as he played with himself.

I propped myself up on my elbows. "I find them fascinating. So delicate, yet so dexterous, and stabilizing." I leaned over to give them another lick and they curled as Royce moaned and worked himself over a little faster. "Would you like some help with that?"

He nodded. I moved and pushed him back on the bed, straddling his waist, then he helped me work his cock back inside of me. I caressed him as we came together a little slower.

Royce's hands caressed my body as I threaded my fingers through his short black hair, his beard, his chest hair. The pace of our bodies coming together was un-rushed. As we looked at each other, we whispered, "I love you," over and over between shallow breaths and kisses, prolonging our pleasure, staying in this sweet moment until our bodies demanded we give in to a pleasurable release.

We slept in our sticky mess until it was time to get up and meet Pete and Marcy for breakfast.

HEALING TOUCH

ROYCE

I had a lot to think about after my birthday party. We were back out on the Gulf, working another week's catch, but my mind wasn't on where to find the fish. The incredible gift from my parents opened so many doors and ideas. All I could think about was the future, and what if?

We could live in the ocean instead of on it. I could learn to live like the waterfolk if we wanted. The boat didn't have to be our life, or more specifically, mine. We could figure out a way to meet my parents from time to time. I knew Pete was ready to take care of the business and the boat. All I'd have to do is sign the paperwork to give him control of everything. The more I thought about it, the more I liked the idea.

But there was Troller's pod to consider. Maybe they weren't after him any longer, or they might not have found him yet. If we lived underwater, Troller could teach me, and then maybe we could help his pod understand they were being lied to. We were both proof.

Troller and I spent our nights talking about these things. However, we agreed to wait until the end of the season so the crew wouldn't worry. If Troller and I decided to leave, Pete and Kristy could set up the next crew together.

I'd set the anchor for the night, and the crew was working hard to get the traps ready for tomorrow. We were halfway through the week but had a quarter of the catch we'd expected. That was squarely on my shoulders.

"Daydreaming again?" Pete asked as he appeared in the nest. He was the only one on the crew that knew what Troller was and about my birthday present. We didn't keep secrets anymore, and I felt better for it.

I sighed. "Maybe I should have you navigating for the rest of the week. I'm off my game. And we don't have nearly enough for wholesale." We wouldn't have to find individual buyers for replication farms or general distribution if we could make our wholesale number, which would give us access to a larger market with an agent to sell for us. Otherwise, I had to do the legwork to get the sales. We only had half of what we needed. It happened sometimes.

"What we have is decent breeding stock, though, good enough for the replication farms. We'll be able to offload what we have, but wholesale would be nice," Pete said. He walked over to me and leaned against the console, facing me. He knew me well enough to know what was distracting me. "Whatever you decide, I'll support you. Kristy and I can handle the boat just fine."

"I know." I rubbed my face and took a deep breath. "I wonder if I've romanticized what it would be like. Maybe I've created this whole idea in my head, and it'll actually be nothing like I imagine."

Pete shrugged. "You're right." I frowned until he continued. "It could be nothing like you imagined, and it could be ten times better than you ever dreamed, Royce. Besides, we can make plans. Set up meeting points. Make sure you and Troller are safe."

"You have a point. After the season is over, we can—" An alarm from the deck went up. Pete and I scrambled out of the nest to find Kristy sitting on the deck, Troller holding her hand while Chris and Jamie grabbed first aid gear. Blood was streaming down Kristy's arm from a wound to her hand.

"Shit." I turned to Pete. "Get on the horn to the Coast Guard and find out how fast they can have an emergency flight out here." Pete turned around and ran back to the nest. Chris and Jamie returned with the medkit. We opened the kit and looked through it for the supplies we needed.

"Kristy, you'll be alright. I've seen a lot worse, okay? When this is over, you'll have a nice scar to show off." The trap she had been prepping for the next day had broken, driving a sharp piece of the frame through her hand.

She gritted her teeth and nodded. "I knew I should have pulled that trap. I thought we might get another round out of it."

"Don't berate yourself. Anyone would have made the same choice. It could have been any of us with a new piercing." She laughed at my half-assed joke as I prepped to clean her wound to see how much damage we were dealing with.

Before any of us could do anything, Troller spoke. "Don't be afraid." He held her wrist and yanked the piece of metal out of it.

"Troller, no!" I reached for him, but I was too late.

Blood poured out of Kristy's wound, and Troller wrapped his hands around hers. A moment later, a blue light formed around Kristy's hand between Troller's. When the light stopped, so had the blood. Troller let go of her hand and it was whole again.

Pete came back. "Coast Guard eta is about an hour. If we can keep her stable." Pete did a double take as Troller used some gauze to wipe blood from Kristy's hand. "What the fuck happened?"

We all sat in a state of shock and watched as Kristy flexed her fingers. We looked at Troller, and no one moved for a long moment. Then I gathered my wits and barked orders.

"Chris, deal with the medkit. Jamie, take Kristy to the galley and make sure she drinks some juice, and watch for signs of shock. Pete, call off the Coast Guard."

Pete went back toward the hatch, then turned around to ask, "What do I tell them?"

"Tell them it wasn't as serious as we first thought, and we'll follow up when we return to port." I stood, looked out across the water, around the boat, and back at Troller. His eyes met mine, and he flinched slightly. I had to have looked upset, though I hadn't meant to point it at him. I had been scared for Kristy, but now I was scared for Troller for a completely different reason.

"Okay." Pete left, and the rest of the crew followed my directions. It left me on deck with Troller, who kept staring at his hands.

I offered Troller my hand, and he reached to take it. His were still covered in Kristy's blood. "Did you know you could do that?" I held his hand as we talked.

He glanced at me, then glanced toward the hatch Kristy and Jamie disappeared into. "I'm not sure. One minute I was staring at her hand, and the next, I knew I could heal it." He shook his head. "Heal isn't the right word. It was more like a wish. I could wish for it to be whole." He looked at the blood on his hands and tried to rub it away. "I saw Halic do something similar when one of our people was hurt."

"But how did *you* know you could do it?" Not that I wasn't grateful, but I didn't want Troller risking himself or members of the crew on a hunch that might cost someone a limb, or worse.

"I had a scratch on my hand the other day." He ran his thumb over his palm. "It was tiny, but it hurt. So I rubbed my thumb over it and wished it would go away, and it did."

I glanced at his hand, not sure what to make of his story.

"While you were sleeping, I saw a scar on your back. What was it from?"

"I fell out of a tree when I was a kid. A branch got me pretty good on the way down." I held onto him as he swayed, not from the motion of the boat.

"I didn't like it, so I wished it away." He looked like he was on the verge of tears. "I hope that's alright. I'm sorry, Royce. I thought I was helping. I couldn't watch Kristy suffer. She looked like she was in so much pain. Please don't be mad, please."

"I'm not mad, Troller. You scared us, is all. We didn't know what you were doing, and when something like that happens, we leave the object in place so we don't make it worse."

"I didn't know that."

"I know." I pulled him in for a hug, and he clung to me. "Come on, let's clean you up. Then we can check on Kristy."

Troller came with me to our cabin but didn't look up once. I sat him on our bed, retrieved a towel, wet it, and brought it back to him. Gently, I took one of his hands and wiped it clean, then started on the other. I was beginning to worry about him. He'd never been so unresponsive before.

"You did the right thing. Even if we didn't understand it. Kristy could have lost the use of her hand."

"I have magic, Royce." Troller's voice was quiet, like he didn't quite believe what he had done.

I tried to give him a smile. "Seems so." I finished cleaning his hands and tossed the washcloth into the dirty clothes hamper. When I looked at him again, a spark of anger was in his eyes.

"Halic isn't the only one. Don't you see what this means?!" Troller jumped up and started pacing our cabin. "What if others in the pod could have magic if they left the water? I've been out of the water for months, and now I can wish things whole. What other magic might our pod have? What else could we do if we only tried, Royce?" He reached out and grabbed my hands. His gaze held an ocean of determination. "The council needs to know. We need to help the pods understand. Halic needs to be stopped."

I pulled him into a hug, and he wrapped his arms around me as he settled onto my lap. "We'll figure it out. I'll help you. I promise."

After we finished cleaning up, we checked on Kristy. She and the other crew were in the galley laughing when we entered. The laughter stopped, and Kristy stood and came over to Troller.

"You saved my hand. Thank you, Troller." She wrapped her arms around him for a hug.

He patted her on the back, then hugged her. "You're my friend, Kristy. I am happy it worked."

The crew relaxed for the night, and everyone had a beer, except Pete. He was in charge of the nest for the evening. When I went to check on him, he was reading something on his phone.

"Everything okay? The Coast Guard was happy they didn't have to come out." Pete stuck his phone back in his pocket.

"Everything is good." I nodded. I took a breath and let it out. "When the season is over, we should talk about what you and Kristy want to do with the business. I think Troller and I are going to take a trip."

Pete grinned. "About time you figured that one out." He patted me on my back, and I chuckled.

"Yeah, yeah. There's still a lot to set up, but I think if we can help Troller's people, we should."

Pete nodded. "We'll figure it out, Royce. Like we always have."

"You're right. As usual." I chuckled and took a sip of my beer.

"I know. It's a hard job, but someone has to keep you honest." We laughed, and I kept Pete company for a while longer until Troller came by and wanted to go to bed. With our future in front of us, I felt pretty good. If Troller and I could save his people and help them return to the surface, then that would be worth giving up my life above the waterline to be with him.

PERFECT STORM

ROYCE

A few days later, I'd planned to move us from one of our regular spots to one that was better populated with our intended catch. If we could grab a few more decent hauls, we could wrap up the season on a high note. The crew was in good spirits, even after what happened with Kristy, so we kept going and tried our luck. I got the short straw and woke up early to move the boat.

It surprised me when Troller woke with my alarm. I'd expected the crew to sleep some this morning, and Pete planned to wake up an hour after me. When I told Troller to go back to sleep, he moved between my legs instead.

His mouth was hot and tight as he wrapped his lips around me. I relaxed into the sensations and the feeling of his tongue and throat that brought me from half-mast to full in no time. In my sleepy, very aroused state, I hadn't noticed that he had nudged my legs open wider. When he pressed a finger into me, I choked with the immediate reaction it got out of my body. I came so hard that it took a few more minutes to focus enough to think about taking a shower and getting dressed. Troller moved up my body and kissed me until I opened my eyes. I felt his hard-on press into my thigh, and I moved a hand to cup him and kiss him back. After a few gentle tugs on his dick, he pushed me away.

"Don't you have to move the boat?"

"Am I the captain or not?"

"You are, but what I want, we don't have time for this morning because you have to move the boat."

I looked at him, feeling my brows furrow and a smile form on my lips. "What did you have in mind, exactly?"

"If I tell you, are you going to get out of bed?"

"Maybe." The likelihood was no. I would do whatever he wanted. Instead, he pushed my hand away again.

"No," Troller said. "Tonight. Promise. Did you like what I did?"

I grinned at him. "Of course I did. I like your nimble fingers and your sexy mouth."

"I thought it would be a nice way to wake you, since you had to be up early." Troller practically purred with his words.

"Did you have more of that planned for later?"

"Maybe."

"I see. Why not right now?"

"Because you have to move the boat, and if you're not up before Pete, he's going to tease us all day about it. I suspect half the reason he's waiting an hour is so he can catch you being late. So," he kissed me gently, "my love." He kissed me more passionately, and I responded, reaching for him, just as he rolled away. "You need to get up. I'll make your coffee."

I laughed and shook my head, and maybe pouted a little, too. Troller put on a robe and left our room to make coffee. I grabbed a quick shower, threw on some clothes, then went to the nest. Troller came by with a cup, fixed exactly the way I liked it, kissed my cheek, and went back to our room.

The replay of earlier was still fresh in my mind when Pete showed up thirty minutes later with a cup of coffee. I already had the boat moving, and if the waves held, we'd make good time arriving at our next spot.

"Morning, Captain," Pete said.

"Morning," I said to him, smiling.

"In all the years we've worked together, I've never seen you smile so much, especially this early."

I shrugged. We both knew why, and there was no point in saying it out loud.

Pete cleared his throat. "Hey, um, I want to chat with you about something."

"Sure, what's up?"

"Um, I talked with Marcy last night."

"And?"

"She's pregnant."

"Congratulations, Pete!" He hadn't mentioned anything about an engagement, but the way he and Marcy were, a baby wasn't that big of a surprise.

"Thanks. We're pretty happy about it, too." He smiled. "Happened the night of your birthday party, if you wanted to know."

I choked on my sip of coffee. "Not really, but alas, now I do," I said, with some playful snark in my voice.

"Oh please, as if we don't know what you two are doing in your cabin, even with the soundproof spells you have. The grin on your face every morning gives you away."

I changed the subject, though I was still smiling. "When is the due date?"

"Near the end of the off-season, I think. I don't remember the date Marcy told me. She's doing fine, though. She had her first checkup, and the doc scheduled imaging for her in a few weeks."

I took a sip of my coffee and waited Pete out. He had something more on his mind. I wondered if this would change his mind about helping me with the business while Troller and I were away.

"Marcy and I would like you and Troller to be the godparents. If that's alright with you and Troller, of course."

"Well, damn." Until Pete said something, I hadn't thought about being a godparent, let alone a parent. I wanted to be with Troller, and I knew he'd be an amazing parent. So much solidified for me at that moment. I could almost kiss Pete for it. Almost. Instead, I put down my coffee cup and reached for him.

He looked confused until I pulled him into a hug and squeezed him until he made a strangled noise.

"Is that a yes, then?" he gasped out.

"Yes. Definitely. And I'm sure Troller will agree to it as well."

"What do I agree to?" Troller asked as he came into the nest. I let go of Pete and turned him around, and pointed him at Troller, who looked like he wasn't sure if he wanted to punch Pete or me. Ever since I mentioned the kiss, he's been playfully jealous of Pete's friendship. We talked about it, and he knew Pete was with Marcy, but even so, Troller had a mild jealous streak.

Truth be told, I liked to poke it a little sometimes. The sex was epic when he was in a possessive mood. I cleared my throat and pointed at Pete, who was still standing in front of me with his hands up like he'd been caught stealing cookies from the galley.

"Pete and Marcy are having a baby, and they want us to be the godparents," I said.

The change that came over Troller was instantaneous. He grabbed Pete up in a similar, air-gasping hug and said yes so many times, and with such excitement, I was almost jealous. Those were my yeses, and I was going to explain that to him later. Maybe right after I parked the boat, with a lot of kissing and hands in places that would make him say yes to me instead.

Troller regained control of himself and let go of Pete. Pete gasped for air and braced himself against the console.

"Well, that's that then. I'll let Marcy know." He coughed a few more times and nodded, then smiled. "I'll go send her a message real quick and be right back."

"Godparents. Royce, that's amazing!" Troller came over to me and gave me a hug. I snuggled him while I checked the course to ensure the boat was still heading in the right direction.

"I have to admit, I like the idea too."

"Are they going to do a binding ceremony?"

"Like a wedding?"

Troller nodded. "Different cultures have different ceremonies. It's a custom among surface dwellers, though not always necessary." It sounded like someone had been doing more research about surface dwellers, as he called us. Which now that I thought about it was probably why he had known what a godparent was.

"I'm not sure. Pete talked about it a while back, but he didn't mention it just now. If they get to that point, I'm sure they'll let us know." Might have to ask Pete myself now that I was curious.

"Good. It would give me an excuse to buy a new dress."

I leaned over and kissed the side of his head, then patted his ass. "Well, before you spend your hard-earned wages, you might want to prepare the deck. We should arrive at our new spot in about thirty minutes."

"Aye, Captain," Troller said before he kissed my cheek. I watched him head back down to the deck, wearing the blue shorts. I was sure now that he was teasing me. Whenever we called it a night, I was definitely peeling him out of those. I sighed and got back to work.

I laid out the grid for the traps and the crew prepped them to drop. We set everything up by noon, broke for lunch, then moved around picking up our traps. We made a decent enough catch for the day that I decided we'd spend the rest of the week in the area, then take our haul in.

Kristy came up to the nest with me toward the end of the day. She looked at the sonar map on the nav station. "Captain, take a look at this. We have a lot of movement below us."

"Oh? What kind of fish are we looking at?"

"I don't think these are fish. They're too big and moving too fast," Kristy said.

The weather instrumentation beeped and indicated the wind had picked up. I looked out over the deck to see clouds rolling in. "That's weird. We were supposed to have clear skies for the next few days."

I saw Troller run across the deck, waving his arms at the nest. I went down to meet him as he hit the bottom of the stairs.

"Royce! We have to go. Now. It's not safe."

"Slow down a minute. It's just a storm rolling in. Nothing we haven't dealt with before."

His voice was harsh. "It's not a storm, Royce. It's my pod. They know I'm here."

"Oh, shit." I scrambled back to the nest, sounded the horn, and got on the loudspeaker. "Stow gear as fast as you can. We're moving as soon as everyone is inside. Haul ass, people! This is not a drill."

Pete gave me a thumbs up from the deck, and Troller went back to help. The team was well-practiced and had the deck cleared and gear stowed in five minutes flat. I had the engines warm and the anchor up as they all came inside. I hit the throttle and moved us around to head into deeper water so we could move faster.

Troller had told me it had been hard catching up to moving boats. I'm sure it was a different story when the ship started from a standstill, and the *Aire Apparent* wasn't small, or as easily maneuverable. Rain hit the boat, and at first nothing seemed odd about it until the first wave hit us hard. I heard my crew screaming.

I pulled the mic and yelled into the loudspeaker. "Get buckled in! Pete! Get your ass up here. I need you on nav."

Pete showed up just as another wave slammed into us. "What the fuck is this shit? There weren't any hurricanes in the forecast."

"Troller's people," I said. Pete looked like he swallowed his tongue but moved to the nav station and gave me headings. We were barely staying ahead of the storm when a wave as big as a skyscraper appeared in front of the boat, poised to drop on top of us, then froze as if someone was holding the water like a large blanket.

I brought the boat to a full stop, slowing the boat to a drift. High-pitched calls echoed around and through the boat. Troller appeared in the nest and I watched him as he looked at the boat-crushing wave. He shook his head and turned to go.

"Where are you going?" I yelled. He went down the steps, and I followed as I called back to Pete, "Take the controls!"

"Troller!" He was standing on deck, facing the wave.

He glanced at me with fear in his eyes. "Royce!"

The storm was soaking us both. I reached for his arm and pleaded. "Troller, go back inside. We can figure something out."

"I can't run anymore, Royce. The calls you heard were for me. They'll destroy this boat to get to me. I can't let that happen."

"I can't lose you, Troller." I wrapped my arms around him. "Please. There has to be another way."

There was an ear-piercing whistle, and both of us dropped to our knees on the deck. When it stopped, we helped each other to our feet and went to the side. A group of Troller's people circled the boat.

The waterfolk were pale compared to the dark blue-greens I was used to seeing on Troller, as if they hadn't been exposed to light in a long time. They seemed to hold their position in the waves with no trouble and stared up at us with the same distinct black eyes Troller had.

The clicks, whistles, and tones sounded like an ultimatum to me. Troller grew still, and I reached for him. He took my hand and turned toward me.

"Royce, no matter what, I love you. I will always, until my last breath, love you. Remember that."

He kissed me, and I grabbed him and kissed him harder. I didn't want to let him go, but when he pulled away, I stood and watched as he took a few steps and leapt over the side, disappearing as his body pierced the water.

Moments later, the wave threatening the boat slid back into the sea, and the rain stopped. Another thirty minutes and it was like nothing had happened, except Troller was gone.

WOVEN REEDS & WORDS

TROLLER

I felt like a stunned fish. To leave Royce like that tore something inside of me. I wasn't sure I'd ever get back. I only hoped he'd forgive me and that he and the crew were safe.

The pod surrounded me the moment I hit the water. I expected them to murder me while I shifted, but they only watched. Once my skin cast-off floated away, they looped woven reeds around my neck and wrists. I pulled, but the ropes held tight as the reeds abraded my gills.

"Is this how you treat a member of the council?" I was pretty sure I didn't have much sway anymore, but I had to try. I saw doubt in the protectors' eyes until Elder Councilor Halic joined them.

Halic projected strength as he moved among us. His blonde-white hair was elaborately woven with many trinkets to denote his status among the pods. He had pale yellow stripes along his sides that matched the color of his upper body, though the rest of his scales were a faint green.

"This is how we treat traitors and those that expose us to the surface dwellers. You will be taken back to the pod and judged for your actions. You no longer have a voice here," said Halic.

Halic swam close to me and clicked in my ear, "You barely look like any of us; you are so tainted from being with the air breathers. Look at you. You disgust me." I knew what he meant. I had more sun. My hair was bright from Royce's potions, and my skin had a healthy glow to it because I had renewed it every so often. It made me wonder how Halic hid his trips to the surface. The protectors that surrounded us had muted colors and dull scales as well. I had never noticed how unhealthy we appeared from our lack of time above the water.

"I frighten you, Halic. There is fear in your eyes, as plain as moss on stone." I didn't keep my sounds quiet as I challenged him. My people needed to know. If I were to face what I'd done and sway those around me, then I would give them the truth.

As I opened my mouth to speak, Halic motioned with his hand and spelled my voice away. I strained to make a noise, but nothing came from my throat. "That will be enough from you, traitor," Halic clicked.

He gave instructions and forced me to keep up. He must have known I would speak about how he had lied and learned magic from the surface. It was the only reason to keep me silent, though I didn't understand why he kept me alive.

In all the time I was with Royce, none of my research mentioned that anyone had seen waterfolk on land or in the water in a long time. There were several pods in the Gulf, but what about other parts of the world? Had all my kind across the seas vanished, or had they retreated deep into the sea to avoid the surface dwellers as we had? Had they left the sea and become surface dwellers themselves? I needed answers, and the only one that might have them was Halic.

They took me to a hollow space in a rock face near where my pod sheltered. It was barely big enough for me to fit. When they shoved me inside, they secured a reed hatch over the entrance and left me to stare out of it.

There was enough room to breathe, but that was all. I could not stretch my arms out, nor could I fit them through the reed hatch. My food comprised half-dead fish and seaweed that would drift by.

I lost track of time until I adjusted to the tides again. Surface dwellers told time with their sun and moon. Things we felt below the waves but rarely saw. When I slept, I dreamed of Royce, his boat, and my blue dress. I keened with my muted voice for my broken heart.

At my lowest point, Halic appeared like flotsam. He had another with him, an adolescent, maybe a little older, but I couldn't be sure. While the light was dim, I could tell the child had a hint of red hair similar to mine.

"Greetings, Troller," Halic vocalized. "This is your replacement, Aisling. She will take over as the councilor for your pod. All you need to do is the proper exchange with me as your witness, and you'll be free of your burden."

Aisling looked frightened. Her gaze shifted between us, possibly wondering who was the greater predator. Halic swam her forward until she neared the reed hatch. She stretched out her small hand toward me. If I could have reassured her, I would have. I tried to smile instead. She smiled back.

Did she know she would continue to perpetuate a betrayal on our people? I wished I could speak with her. I hadn't realized I'd looked away until she spoke. Her soft clicks and sounds made my heart hurt.

"It is alright, Councilor Troller. I will help our people. Elder Halic has explained to me that the surface dwellers have poisoned your mind. So you can rest well knowing that I will see to our pod," Aisling vocalized. She reached out again, waiting for me to take her hand and acknowledge the transfer of power.

I shook my head and pushed myself away from the hatch. The child looked distraught. If Halic wanted me to give up my leadership, he'd have to kill me. I would not willingly put a child Halic could use to his own end in my place.

"Come Aisling. We will try again when Troller is more agreeable. Perhaps after a few more days without a proper meal." Halic clicked.

He meant to starve me then. So be it. I moved my fin and circulated the water in my cell. Wherever Royce was, I hoped he was alright.

TORN LOYALTIES

ROYCE

My head felt like someone had taken a brick to it. No, not a brick, a tranquilizer. Fucking Pete.

I laid in my cabin, remembering some of what happened. Everyone searched for Troller or any signs of his pod. After an hour of nothing, I was determined to do something about it and put the tender into the water. When Pete asked me what I was doing, I remember giving him instructions to take the *Aire Apparent* back and leave me there.

He argued about having a better plan, food, water, concern for the crew, for the boat. I didn't care about any of it. All I knew was that I needed to find Troller before they could hurt him. After that, it was lights out.

It was dark in my room, and my mind wandered a bit, still groggy from the tranquilizer. Troller was gone, and if Pete had moved the boat, any hope I had of finding him went with it. There was a chime at my door to let me know someone wanted to enter. I didn't care. It cracked open a bit, and I groaned at the intrusion of light from the hallway.

"Hey Royce, you awake yet?"

Pete. I wanted to both strangle and thank him. He'd looked out for the crew, and the boat when I'd lost my mind, and the other half of my soul. He did the right thing. Someday I might accept that, but my heart couldn't. Not right now.

"Lucky we had those tranq darts, huh? Here we were worried about sharks and dolphins hurting themselves in the trap lines, and it turns out I had to calm my knuckle head of a captain. It took two of them to knock you out."

I huffed. I wanted him to leave, but as usual, Pete was persistent.

"Maybe I should write to the fishing regulation board and suggest an alternate use. I'm sure they'd want to come up with guidelines or something, right?"

"Fucking stop, Pete. Why are you in here?"

"Well, Captain, I wanted to let you know we are back at our home port. I've offloaded what we had, paid the crew through the end of the season, and dismissed them. Plus, Marcy brought pastries." He shook the pink box as if it was a baited line.

I sat up slowly and groaned. Pete took that as permission and came in. My head hurt. He put down the pastry box on my bed, pulled a few pills from his pocket, removed a metal water bottle he had slung over his shoulder and offered them to me.

"Thanks." I took them, swallowed the pills, and drank from the bottle until I thought I would puke. When Pete turned to pick up the pastry box again, I noticed the tranq dart gun in his waistband.

"What the fuck did you bring that for?"

"Just in case you did something stupid again, like jumping into the Gulf with no gear and no help."

"Pete, you don't—"

"Understand? Fuck you, Royce. I get it. I lost a friend out there too! I couldn't stand by and lose another because he'd lost his fucking mind with grief for five minutes. I understand, and I would have done the same thing if it was Marcy. You don't have to explain it to anyone, least of all me." Pete settled on the bed next to me and offered the pastry box. I took it and mindlessly ate one. It tasted like ash.

Tears slipped down my face before I realized it. The box slipped from my hands and hit the floor. I covered my face, embarrassed, scared, and angry with my actions and for what might happen to Troller.

"I got a fix on where we were," Pete said quietly. "Before I moved the boat."

I slowly looked up at him.

"You have a starting point."

I frowned, then shook my head, finally remembering the potion. Fuck, I'd been so angry and scared that I'd completely forgotten about it until now. I launched across the bed and pulled the wood box out of the storage Troller had stashed it in.

"Is that what you were going to use so you could go with Troller?" Pete asked.

"Yeah. It works as long as I stay in the water. I forgot about it when everything happened."

We were both quiet for a minute. "I . . ." We both tried to talk, and I nodded for Pete to go first.

"I'm not sorry. I kept you from hurting yourself. If you're mad at me for that, I can live with it."

"No, I'm not mad."

He gave me a look as if he didn't believe that, so I amended my statement.

"Well, I'm less mad about it now. You kept me from doing something half-assed. Kept the crew safe. I'm grateful, Pete."

Pete nodded. "Now, let's get resupplied and head back out. With your little potion here, we can do recon and find your merman." He patted me on the back and stood.

"Maybe you should stay here, Pete."

He turned to look at me. "What are you talking about?"

"I don't know how dangerous it's going to be or how long it will take. Marcy's pregnant. If something happened to you, I wouldn't forgive myself." Our gazes met for a moment in the silence as Pete thought about what I said.

He shook his head. "You need help, you bonehead. Maybe you hit your head too hard on the deck when you dropped. I'm going with you."

"I need you to help me by taking care of the boat." I pointed at the floor for emphasis and then at him for good measure. "And your partner and the child you two made, asshole. Don't make this harder than it already is."

"Oh, that was a low blow, even for you. Marcy would box my ears if I let you do this by yourself, and she has more stamina than both of us put together. We love each other, but she would lose all respect for me if I let you do this alone."

I shook my head again. "Fine, Pete, you win."

He looked surprised. "We're done arguing?"

I nodded. "Why don't we go look at the coordinates and make plans to resupply?" I stood. He had a smile on his face. I cringed inwardly.

"I'm glad you see it my way." Pete turned back toward the door. "I thought for a minute I might have to call your parents."

He was too slow to realize I'd grabbed the dart gun. When the dart hit him in the ass, he barely had time to say ouch before he tumbled forward. I caught him before he pancaked on the floor.

I pulled the dart and put Pete on my bed. I used my phone to message Marcy and let her know to meet us at the boat later for dinner. That way, she'd find Pete and help him. I grabbed the potion and went up to the nest, checked the nav, and saw that we were over three hundred kilometers from the location Pete had marked. I grabbed one of the dive computers that had a sophisticated topographical and geo location, then plugged in the coordinates. It would help me navigate underwater. It might not get me the whole way, but it was a start.

I tried to think of anything else I'd need. I messaged Pete's phone, so he'd have instructions and where he could find the paperwork that would let him operate and take care of the business in my absence.

The anguish I felt at whether to tell my parents about what happened was a lump in my throat. I closed my eyes for a minute while I took a breath. When I opened them, I sent a message to Leo.

< Hey, Papa. My birthday present is going to come in handy. Troller and I are taking some time off the boat. If you need anything, Pete's in charge until we get back. Love you, and give my love to Pop. >

I dropped my phone into the captain's seat, looped the dive computer around my wrist, and picked up the bottle. When I got to the deck, I ditched all my clothes and jumped into the water, swimming away from the boat as much as I thought was safe. If this potion went wrong, I hoped I could swim back.

I broke the seal, waited for it to change color, and downed the whole goopy mess. It tasted weird, like too much snot in the back of your throat. I waited, treading water. Nothing happened. Then pain shot up my back, and I gasped for air as I sank under the surface.

When I woke, I was on the seafloor breathing as if I'd always lived there. I had the bottle in one hand and the dive computer in the other. I looked at myself. Claws, webbed fingers, large fluke, hip fins, and a slit. While Troller looked more like a Spanish mackerel—ice blue to dark blue with dots—I had the black patterned stripes and fins that seemed to match a bonito.

"No way," I heard myself click. Seems I had an unfamiliar voice, too. I could make the same sounds as Troller, though whether they meant anything was a different story. I poked at my genital pouch with my fingers, amused, and wondered what Troller would think. My fascination ended there. Determination set in.

I looked at the dive computer and flipped it on. It gave me a ping and a general direction. I flipped it off and tried to swim in that direction. Moving with a fin was much harder than I thought. The first few times I propelled myself forward, I twisted and turned so fast I got disoriented. It took a few more tries to make slow, steady progress.

Hang on, Troller. I'm on my way.

SACRIFICES

Troller

Time had no meaning as I grew weaker. My gills hurt. The protectors checked on me, and a few showed mercy. They left food when they could and would give me news about the pod.

One night, a protector showed up with a large gash in their fluke that made it hard for them to swim. I don't know if they incurred the injury from a boat or from a larger predator.

I was still mute, but I motioned to them. They came close enough for me to see that the protector was unmated, and had multiple scars from injuries.

"Greetings, Councilor Troller. My name is Phyris."

The protector was new, but seemed kind. I stuck my fingers through the reed hatch and tried to motion him closer, but he hesitated.

"I don't understand, Councilor Troller."

I was desperate to help Phyris. He was a member of my pod, and I didn't want to see him suffer. I motioned to my arm and ran my fingers along it, mimicking the path of another scar he carried.

"My scar? Would you like to hear how I got it?" he clicked. I didn't miss the bravado in his song. I might be trapped, but waterfolk were a people that admired stories and scars alike. If one involved the other, even better.

Instead, I made another hand motion to draw him close and touched my arm.

"You want to touch my scar?"

Even though his vocalizations held some surprise, his body language told me he thought I was flirting with him. I gave a nod of agreement. Flirting or not, if I could show him he could be healed, maybe the information would spread, and people would ask questions. It needed to if I had any hope of removing Halic.

Phyris held up his arm for me to touch. No sooner had I placed three fingers on his scar, my magic flared to life. The noise he made would have put a youngling to shame.

"My scar! Why did you remove it? How did you remove it?" I backed away from his onslaught of questions. While my hand wouldn't fit through a hole in the hatch, his spear could. He swam in an agitated manner, clicking to himself, clearly upset. When he swam back toward me, he didn't stop until he pressed his face to the hatch. "Councilor Troller, do you have magic?"

I nodded and motioned again to my arm and the place where Phyris's scar was, and then brought my hands together to make a fluke. I repeated this until Phyris backed away from the hatch.

"You want to heal my fluke?"

Yes, by the sea, let me help you. I emphatically nodded. When Phyris presented his fluke, it filled me with hope. The gash was newer than the scar, but it was more severe. Phyris pressed his fluke to the hatch, and I laid my hand on the scarred area.

Moments later, Phyris swam away, fully healed. His joyous clicks amused me as I watched him swim. My lack of sustenance made the magic use draining, causing my eyes to close as exhaustion set in. Phyris noticed and swam to the hatch.

"Are you hungry?"

I gave him a sleepy nod.

"I'll bring you sustenance, Councilor." The adoration in his clicks might have amused me before, but now it reminded me of Royce. When Phyris swam away, I closed my eyes and dreamed of dancing with my prince. Phyris returned with an assortment of shellfish, which I devoured as quickly as he could pass them to me. Once I had finished the entire feast, I drifted off with a full belly for the first time since returning to the water.

After my demonstration to Phyris, others sought me out. Some were guardians with podlings that had a broken limb that healed wrong or protectors with injuries and scar tissue, which inhibited movements.

One pod member wanted me to heal marks clearly given to them by a lover. They were mated with a protector the last time I saw them. When I asked why they wanted them removed, they were reluctant, but finally told me that the protector had found another mate. It wasn't uncommon for protectors to have multiple mates, but it seemed this new dynamic had not worked as they had hoped. I healed them, if only for their peace of mind. I could do nothing about the unseen marks their heart carried.

All of them thanked me with food. It was enough. I counted the days by the rotation of the protectors assigned to watch me, and the direction change of the currents. The same ones surface dwellers called tides. None of them stopped anyone that came to me for help. Word was spreading.

It was almost a week, as surface dwellers would reckon it, before unwelcome vocalizations woke me.

"I've heard stories, Troller." Halic swam closer to the hatch. "You have magic?" He made a hand motion, and I felt my throat change.

"What do you care, Halic?" I vocalized with harsh clicks.

Halic made a soft whistle. "Don't be so modest, Troller. You learned from someone. An air breather, perhaps? Did they teach you?"

"No." I wouldn't give Halic a reason to look for Royce. Whatever he thought, I had to dissuade him of the idea that Royce or anyone else on the *Aire Apparent* was involved. "No one taught me. It manifested on its own."

"You're lying. They have magic. We all know that. You either learned it or stole it from them."

"Is that how you learned your magic, Halic? Did you steal it from a surface dweller?" I queried.

Halic motioned to someone I could not see. When a guardian came into view with an egg in their arms, I wasn't sure why at first.

"Show us your magic, Troller. Heal this hatchling, and I'll do what I can to make sure the council is lenient."

There was something behind this request, especially with Halic involved. The hatchling had toes instead of a fluke. If they hatched, they would not survive for long. Other hatchlings, misshaped like this, slowly drowned, not because of the lack of fluke, but because they could not breathe underwater.

I finally recognized it for what it was. The deformity wasn't genetic. It was our other form. If this egg was above the water when it hatched, it would shift and survive. How many podlings had we lost because we were afraid of the surface? I couldn't bring myself to think about it without keening for them.

"Troller, my patience grows thin. Heal the hatchling or face consequences."

The guardian pushed the egg up to the reed hatch, and I placed my hands on the egg as much as I could, determined to wish them into a form that would save their life. Saddened that we were all forced into this charade instead of acknowledging what was right in front of us. Proof that we weren't meant to stay below the surface forever.

A light formed around the small one, and when it faded, the podling had shifted to its underwater form. The guardian swam off with fear in their eyes, not for the egg, but for me. Halic reached for the reed hatch, opened it, then placed his hand on my arm. I felt a jolt, then everything went dark.

Sometime later, I woke in a larger room inside the pod caves, about the same size as Royce's cabin. The caves had been a safe haven for waterfolk well before I was hatched. They were a warren of tunnels and recesses, carved long ago by a volcano. The sleeping nook, the soft moss on the upper cave walls, and various handholds were additions. Someone had lived in this space before they brought here me.

As I became more aware of my surroundings, I noticed that another reed hatch barred the entrance. It was unusual for such things to exist. Before I left, the pod had nothing like doors. Cave-in's happened and privacy was not much of a consideration when sound carried on the currents. We always considered it strange that surface dwellers blocked their passageways. Though now, because of what I learned about boats, doors made sense. But they had no place in the pod caves.

The entrance had a width and height slightly longer than my length, from head to fluke. When I pressed myself to the hatch, I saw another protector near the entrance. She noticed me, and her face betrayed her concern.

"Fear not. I mean no harm." My clicks were rough, but she understood me. I received a small nod before panic laced her features, then stilled, as if a predator drew near.

It was the only warning I had before Halic arrived with Aisling. "As you can see, Troller, I keep my word. The council has decided that you shall remain confined for the rest of your days here instead of banishment. You endangered the pod, and that cannot go unpunished. However, your ability will make up for your recklessness. You will attend to those that need healing, and in exchange, the pod will feed you."

"You couldn't explain it, could you? And you couldn't very well tell them how I gained my magic because then they would question how you gained yours." If I was to remain confined, I was determined not to make it easy for Halic.

"You lie," Halic vocalized with a click and a hiss. "You stole your magic while I was born to such gifts and have only sought to help our people." He motioned for Aisling to come forward. "As part of your punishment, you will teach this one your magic."

"And what if I'm unable to do so?" I vocalized.

"Then you will be punished until you comply." Halic flipped around and swam away.

"Halic." He stopped and looked at me. "I see the fear in your eyes."

I watched as Halic's fluke twitched slightly. He turned back, swam to the hatch, and made a vicious hand motion that stole my voice again. I should have left well enough alone, but I couldn't help myself. Halic swam away. Aisling gave me a brief glance before she followed him.

Something important happened with the council. More than Halic was vocalizing. Why keep me alive if he had the same magic? As a council member myself, if they had presented me with my story, I wouldn't be so quick to throw away my abilities. I would want to see if we could teach others. Maybe I had allies on the council that hadn't made themselves known yet.

Even if there were members of the council aligned with me, I couldn't wait for them to rally. I was forming a plan. One that involved Aisling, if she was willing. Maybe if I could convince her, help her learn the truth, she would help me tell others. If it took years, and cost me my last breath, it would be worth it to help my people into the light.

OVERWHELMED

Royce

Everything was so complicated without Troller. I had to learn how to swim again. I avoided talking with anything that swam past me. When I spoke, my clicks scared them. A pod of dolphins toyed with me until I charged one of them. After that, they gave up. It might have been a territorial issue, but I didn't care. All I wanted was to find Troller. With each passing day, I wondered if I'd survive at all.

Troller had been right about one thing—you lose track of time under the water. The dive computer kept a running dive log every time I turned it on. I'd saved the battery as much as I could, using it sparingly. After a week, the battery gave out. The small compass set into the dive computer housing was the only useful thing left on the device, otherwise it was reduced to an awkward bludgeoning tool.

Catching my first fish took me days. Crabs were easier, but not by much. I found oysters once and ate my fill learning how to use my teeth and claws. They were handy for things like piercing skin and cracking open shells. I idly wondered what my parents would have thought. Would they recognize me? Would Troller?

I stuck to the coastline or within sight of the drop-off that led to the shore. It was far enough out that swimmers didn't see me, but close enough not to be hit by a boat or recreational craft. Or at least, I thought so. Without the buoys and markers I was used, I was mostly guessing and horribly slow.

When I finally found waterfolk, they were friendly at first, but the minute I opened my mouth, they swam away. For the hundredth thousand time I grew frustrated with myself and had so much sympathy for what Troller had endured. It must have been incredibly lonely for him when he left. Avoiding others, hiding, swimming from port to port.

After a month of swimming, catching my food, finding places to sleep when I was tired, and scaring off anyone that might help me because I didn't know how to communicate, I gave up. My heart and spirit were broken. My only hope was that maybe someday Troller would come find me like he had the first time.

I swam for the surface to get my bearings and look for a beach. My plan was to change back and contact Pete. Hopefully no one would recognize me in the meantime. My parents certainly didn't need the publicity.

Within a meter of the surface, I was so focused on swimming up that I hadn't realized I was in danger. With no time to react, a water craft gave me a glancing blow. It was enough to knock my lights out. My last thoughts were of Troller and that no one would ever find me as I sank to the bottom of the sea.

Thankfully, I was wrong. Someone found me. I woke staring into small eyes and a small face with a poof of hair drifting with the current. The child reminded me of Kristy for a moment.

I smiled at them. The child stared, then immediately started screeching. I clapped my hands over my ears, then realized that was pointless as sound traveled much differently through water. I instead clamped my hand over their mouth. That did the trick until I saw an adult swimming above me. They didn't look too pleased, and I let go of the small one who quickly swam behind the adult.

"Sorry," I squawked. The adult winced. I frowned, knowing the right sounds weren't coming out of my throat.

Several more children appeared with the adult in the cave we seemed to occupy. When I tried to move from a horizontal position to a vertical one, I became disoriented and tried to hold my head in a fruitless attempt to make it stop. The children started vocalizing loudly, and the adult pushed me down onto a rock. I wondered if I'd done this before, but couldn't remember.

The adult, who had rows of small braids in their hair and deep indigo skin, darker than Troller's, came back and handed me a fish. I nodded my thanks and ate. They returned a little later and gave me another fish, and I ate that too. It surprised me that I had no difficulty swallowing in my prone position. I stayed put to ease my vertigo and let the family take care of me until I could take care of myself.

I don't know how much time passed, but I rested and ate. The children became less frightened of me. They brought me things for my beard, longer now than it had been than when I'd left the boat. Shells, rocks, pieces of smooth glass. They braided them into my hair and I used them to communicate. I would tap on the objects, and they would verbalize the name. Or at least I hoped that was the case.

A breakthrough came about when one of them pointed at a shell in my beard, then made a noise, then pointed at themselves and made the same vocalization. I repeated it, and they looked pleased. After that, I learned all five of the children's names.

Though I had no idea what they meant in English, I repeated the sounds for their names, and in my head made up names to match the sounds—Shell, Button, Hoof, Tremble, and Yucky. They would make delighted noises, and their parent, Garden, would smile at me sometimes. I also learned fish, seaweed, teeth, fin, fingers, claws, and a host of other words. The children were delighted to teach me, and I was grateful to learn.

The parent asked me my name, and I tried to sound it out the way Troller had taught me. The family all looked surprised, but nodded. I didn't know what that meant, but Garden repeated it back, and that sound became my name. One day, I was brave enough to say Troller's name. That received a very different reaction.

Garden vocalized a story's worth of information, but all I understood was my name and Troller's. When the children joined the conversation, I gave up and smiled, listening to the family converse.

When it was clear I could swim again without disorientation, Garden and the children led me out of their cave. We swam for a while until we reached another series of caves. They pointed at a group of waterfolk. I hadn't realized there was such a size difference. Garden was about Troller's length. These other waterfolk were larger, had more muscles, and were longer from head to tail. Garden took me up to them and conversed. They vocalized my name and looked at me. Garden pointed to my head, and they nodded in agreement.

I was pretty sure they thought the boat had knocked me hard enough that I couldn't vocalize properly any longer. I had no way of changing their minds, but the larger waterfolk took charge of me. Before Garden left, they hugged me and vocalized softly, and whatever they said seemed like parental concern. When they let me go and swam away, they rotated onto their back to wave goodbye. I waved to them, grateful for their help and worried about what was next.

This new group took me into their cave system and gave me what amounted to a shelf to sleep on. I was told when to wake up, when to eat, and when to sleep. I followed the routine, and I figured out quickly that I was some kind of guard, but who we guarded or why wasn't apparent. I stayed with the group and learned more vocalizations. I heard my name everywhere, which I thought was odd. Was everyone talking about me?

I made friends with another guard I named Purple. He was nice enough and tried to explain things to me. I eventually had enough vocabulary to ask him about my name.

"Why say, Royce? My name is Royce," I vocalized.

"Your name isn't councilor." Purple shook his head. "You protect the councilors and the pod."

"Protect Royce?"

"Yes, you protect councilors. Or watch over them, like Councilor Troller."

I caught Troller's name, my name, and protection. "Royce Troller?"

"Yes, Councilor Troller."

I pointed at my eyes and said, "Royce Troller" again.

"No one sees Councilor Troller." The guard shook his head and vocalized something else I didn't understand.

I gritted my teeth. It was frustrating to know Troller was somewhere close by, but I couldn't see him. If I understood correctly, the guard said no one saw him or had seen him. I was close, though. I had to be.

Hallucinations

Troller

When I was taken by Halic to our pod's birthing fields, I used my magic to shift some newer developing eggs into their underwater forms. I kept track of the ones I transformed. There were eight partially shifted hatchlings. Eight out of twenty.

If my people knew we could take the eggs to the surface to help them, I wouldn't need to use my magic. The Halic couldn't use my pod's desperation against them. The eggs could have hatched on a protected beach. It would let the podlings learn how to shift in their own time instead of my magic forcing them to while they were at their most vulnerable.

Thankfully, as time passed, Halic hadn't forced me to procreate because of my magic. I had heard it discussed several times by others while we were in the birthing fields who wished they had magic, too. When I left my pod, I hadn't been all that keen on it. Now, I couldn't imagine raising a life without Royce.

When I thought about it, I grew angry, then vocalized something offensive to Halic. He would mute me for it, again and again. He became more suspicious of my influence as the protectors around me grew sympathetic. Halic always controlled my access to the pod and limited my communications when he desired it. I rarely had a moment to vocalize my grievances properly.

In my room, I spent time practicing my languages, writing them on the sandy floor. On one wall, I kept track of the days and months like a surface dweller, converting the current shifts as best I could without the sun and moon. It had been six months since they forced me from the surface, as best I could tell.

Shortly after my seventh month under water, the Midyear feast arrived. It marked the beginning of abundance. On the surface, it marked the beginning of the fishing season.

I hadn't realized it until I had spent time above the water that the surface dwellers had changed their fishing practices to protect the seas and oceans. Royce and his crew were some of the few that were allowed to fish and live trap new stock, ensuring that there was enough for those that lived in the water. My pod and several others had benefited from this change without knowing it.

For these occasions, instead of being difficult, I let them dress me up and escort me to the feast. I sat politely next to Halic and Aisling as our people ate and swam in intricate patterns. It made me remember the time on the boat when I danced with Royce. I missed cake, and I missed Royce most of all. My heart ached for him and my friends.

As a councilor, even an imprisoned one, I gave the proper words with a pleasant hum in my vocalizations and a polite face. I knew I was slowly succumbing to my predicament when I thought I saw a protector with dark hair and a beard.

Having facial hair was not unheard of, though unusual among waterfolk. When I glimpsed the same protector again, they reminded me of Royce. Hope swam to the surface as I swam to get a better view and watched as he disappeared down a passage away from the main celebration.

My fluke put me into motion before I could think about what I was doing. I had to know. Was I so distraught and complacent that I hallucinated Royce? If he was in the pod caves, wouldn't he have found me by now?

"Royce, Royce!" I vocalized. He knew his name. I'd taught him. If it was him, he would hear me. "Royce!"

In my weakened state, my assigned protectors easily caught me. Halic apologized to the gathering and made excuses about how I needing to rest my mind. The moment we were out of sight of those at the feast, Halic stole my voice again. I bared my teeth and gave him a soundless hiss of anger.

"Do you miss your air breather? He's not coming to save you, Troller. You should resign yourself to that." His cruel vocalizations cut deep. I vowed to strangle Halic if I ever had the chance.

In my room, I couldn't let go of the image I saw. A protector with black hair and a beard, broad shoulders, who moved slower than the others and didn't move naturally, as if swimming was learned instead of instinctual.

I shook my head at my foolishness. Pete wouldn't have let Royce do something so reckless, and his parents would have stopped as well. I keened mutely. The silence was unnerving. I didn't even have the solace of my own cries to soothe my heart.

After the Midyear feast, Halic changed his tactics. He allowed Aisling to visit me alone. If Halic suspected my resolve was breaking, he was close to being right. I fantasized what it would be like to let Aisling be councilor and leave to find Royce. Every time I thought about it, my soul felt torn. My chest hurt and my mental state deteriorated more.

Now that I could get a proper look at her, I realized Aisling couldn't have been more than a late adolescent. She always vocalized softly and spoke about Halic with reverence. She didn't have the willfulness or rebellious streak I had at her age. I wished I could tell her everything I knew, but it wasn't to be when she came to me with the news.

"Troller!" She said my name with a pretty trill as the protectors let her into my room. I smiled as she came near and gave her a slight bow. She returned it.

The first few times we had met, she had tried to touch or hug me. I always saw the disappointment in her eyes, however small, when I refused the contact. I knew she meant well. However, I couldn't take the chance that they would see our embrace as some kind of blessing to have her take my place as councilor. It was Halic I didn't trust, and Aisling would likely go along with anything he said.

"Troller, I have met my mate!"

I smiled, happy for her. If it had been different circumstances, I would have hugged her. Finding a mate was an auspicious time.

She swam in excited circles while she vocalized. "He is from another pod and his voice is melodic, and he is so gentle. Halic introduced us and wants us to mate as soon as I'm ready."

So that's why Halic hasn't pushed me to mate. I was almost thankful. If I wasn't so terrified for Aisling, I might have been happier. She was so young and easily manipulated. I feared that this pairing was yet one more way Halic would control her. I wondered how many other council members were in similar situations.

"Isn't it wonderful?" she practically sang.

I tried to be happy for her sake, but I couldn't. Maybe it was better for her to see me sad rather than compliant. Maybe then she might use reason and trust Halic less. At this point, I wasn't sure.

"Troller, you're not happy for me?"

I looked at her and shook my head. I put my hands over my heart and made a reed breaking motion. She clicked in surprise.

"You worry about my heart?"

I nodded. It was close enough that I didn't mime more for her to understand.

"I wish Halic would quit taking your voice. How am I to learn anything if you can't speak with me properly?"

I nodded again. At least that was the right question.

"I will speak with him. This muteness has gone on long enough."

I did not move. I should have stopped her and figured out a way to convey that she should not ask for my voice. But I didn't, for selfish reasons. Maybe the young girls' pleas would get through to Halic. I doubted it, but it was worth a try.

Aisling didn't return for a week. When I finally saw her, she wasn't allowed to see me without her own protector as a shadow. She seemed a little distant, and in poor spirits.

"How are you, Troller?"

I nodded and gave her a soft smile. She returned it. Instead of clicking and vocalizing excitedly about her adventures, or her mate, she set up a stone game on one of the flat surfaces. The point of the game was to use the webbing between your fingers to move the stones in specific patterns. Patterns scored points. I hadn't played in a long time.

Aisling was a natural. Inside that quiet-voiced individual was a talented, keen mind. I held my anger until she left. I punched the stone walls until my hands bled. The protectors stopped me from mangling my hands completely.

"Councilor Troller, you must not hurt yourself so. Your people need you," one of them said.

I tried to wail. I tried making any sound, but all that happened was a violent tremor through my whole body. They worried I would lose my healing magic if I continued. One of them caught me up and placed me on my sleeping shelf. My people. I looked at them and covered my face.

"What can we do for you, Councilor Troller?"

I gaped like a fish trying to breathe. I did not want them to come to harm and risked asking for the only thing that might quiet my mind and my spirit. There was a tuber that grew near hot vents. I drew the shape on the floor and the protectors recognized it. We used the tubers for medicinal purposes to induce sleep and vivid dream states. A day or two later, one of them handed me a small packet of seaweed. The tubers were inside. I smiled at the protector and she smiled in return.

"I wish you peaceful rest, Councilor Troller," she vocalized.

At first I was careful to not take too much. I wanted to be alert for when Aisling arrived so we could play our games. As the visits became a blur and more protectors brought me tubers, or extra food or special colored rocks thought to calm the spirit, the more I let myself sleep instead of eating or playing games with Aisling. In my dreams, Royce was there.

When I woke, I only remembered the nightmare I'd created for myself. Halic found out, of course. It had taken time, but when he came for me at the next birthing cycle, he knew I wasn't of sound mind. I barely stayed awake. He did something with his magic to force me into alertness.

"You disappoint me, Troller. Escaping into dreams? You think it would be that easy? Even mute, you've caused me problems."

He gave me my voice, and I said nothing.

"Have you become an actual mute now? How ironic. Come, it's time for you to visit the birthing grounds again."

I went, and I did my work. I saved five of the fifteen new eggs in the birthing fields. They returned me to my room. The reed hatch shut. They had removed everything except the moss on my sleeping stone. I floated onto its soft surface and buried my face in my arms.

A new protector I'd not seen before guarded me. One with dark hair and a beard. I had to be hallucinating, exhausted or both. It wasn't until I heard my name clicked softly that I recognized the voice.

I replied anyway. There was no harm in talking to a hallucination. "Royce?"

"Troller?" the hallucination clicked my name.

"Please, ghost, don't torment me now. You're nicer when I sleep."

"Up, Troller. Go. We go."

That jarred me. The hand on my arm was familiar, and the sounds were off. In my dreams, Royce spoke clearly in English.

"Troller. It's Councilor. I here. Up," he clicked harshly.

I opened my eyes and Royce was in fact there, and looked like a waterfolk. He had the same dark hair, but it was long, and his beard had trinkets woven into it. However, his face was the same. Even in this form, I knew it was him.

I launched myself at him, and he caught me. His lips were magic, and I felt alive for the first time in a while. He groaned, and I responded as well, then he pulled back a moment as we floated. He smiled, then took my hand and swam us toward the door. I stopped his forward motion. He looked back at me.

I shook my head. "We can't leave, Royce. There's too much at stake."

He shook his head and pulled.

"Who's Royce?"

It was my turn to smile and shake my head. "That's you." I pointed at him.

"Not councilor?"

I shook my head and vocalized his name again. Royce smacked his head. "It's alright, I'll help you." I motioned for him to follow me. I took my finger and wrote words I hadn't used in a long time into the sand.

"I love you."

He smiled, and it was everything to me. My heart felt like it would burst free of my chest. Maybe all was not lost.

The next sentence I wrote was, "We can't leave."

It destroyed that smile faster than any hurricane. We spent a frustrating night trying to communicate. Once I'd explained everything I could, I pushed him outside the door. I could see the pain in his eyes as the new protectors arrived, and they excused him from his duty.

With Royce here, we had a chance to make things right.

THIN PATIENCE

Royce

Since I had arrived and worked with Purple, the guards had become more agitated. They talked about someone being kept and how they wanted to keep them happy.

The guards wouldn't repeat this individual's name and became more secretive. They would vocalize around me, mainly because they thought I didn't understand. They were right, but I kept trying. I knew something was going on when the guards feared one particular waterfolk with long white hair, yellow stripes along his sides, and green scales down his fin. I took to calling him Asshole even though the vocalization of his name didn't sound like that.

One day, Asshole arrived. Several of the guards pointed at me, and I stayed in place. I didn't know what would happen, but Asshole motioned for me to follow him. Purple nodded at me. I trusted Purple, so I went with Asshole. We swam in silence until we reached a room with a reed hatch. I understood "watch and guard" quickly enough. It was all I'd done since I arrived here. With a place to sleep, food, and the occasional mention of Troller's name, I hoped that I'd be able to find him by now, but my patience grew thin.

When I looked into the room I'd been told to guard, I couldn't believe my eyes. Troller was curled up on his sleeping platform. He thwarted my rescue attempt almost immediately, and we spent the night talking about what he'd learned, his pod, his successor, who Halic, aka the Asshole, was and why Troller had to stay.

Troller made sure I took my place before the next shift arrived with the change of the current. While my instincts told me we should swim away as fast as we could, I knew it would break Troller to leave again. Even if it would give him a future, he wouldn't do it, not at the cost of his pod.

The next night, we waited until the passage was clear before I slipped into his room.

We didn't talk; we kissed and continued kissing until Troller swam us to his platform. As long as he kept touching and kissing me, I didn't care where we swam to. He floated mere centimeters above me. It was enough for him to slip a hand between us and then slip his fingers into my genital pouch. The sound I made must have been loud, because Troller's other hand landed over my mouth, quickly muting me. I focused on him, and he smiled.

"Do you remember?" he queried softly. Taking his hand from my mouth, he pointed at his head.

I understood by the gesture, and the meaning was clear by the way he touched me. When his fingers stopped teasing me, I felt bereft. It didn't last long as he pushed himself into my slit, and I tried not to move. Fuck, it was tight. His cock pressed next to mine. It had been too long. There were handholds on the platform I hadn't noticed until Troller reached for them above me. I put my hands on Troller's hips.

He put a finger up to his mouth. "Stay quiet," he clicked. I understood. He pulled slightly, and I pushed at his hips, and it took everything I had not to come.

"Troller," I crooned. The amused clicking made me open my eyes. The experience differed greatly from the previous time. Troller didn't have to breathe for me, and the water played a more significant part in what was happening.

My human skin had only registered temperature changes and the general flow of water. What my body understood now was a whole other experience. Troller's movements made the water caress me all over. The play along my scales and skin teased erogenous places humans didn't have.

It made sense that waterfolk would use the surrounding environment in their lovemaking. I didn't have the words in either language to explain the sensations. It was more than the friction between our genitals. The experience surrounded and completely permeated my being.

Each thrust, fin movement, and brush of my scales Troller made with his body brought me to a hard climax. My whole body writhed with sensation, then again and again until I lost track. Troller filled my pouch with his seed repeatedly, and it mingled with mine. We stayed like that, connected, floating together. When he finally slipped free of me, I had the odd sensation of feeling full and empty at the same time.

At Troller's direction, we adjusted our positions so that I could hold him. His dorsal side to my front. When he rolled, I noticed he had marks on his lower back and across his dorsal ridge from my claws.

"I hurt you," I vocalized with a sad trill the podlings had taught me. Though I couldn't have said I was all that sorry about it. To see him marked by me satisfied some darker part I hadn't been aware of until now. If I'd caused him physical discomfort, I didn't like that aspect.

He turned his head to look at me with a broad smile, like he knew what I was thinking. "We call them lover's marks. No shame. I would do the same. Too much risk to you." Of being discovered, he meant. They paid less attention to him.

When I returned to the protector's sleeping area, I noticed most of them had marks on their hips, back, and buttocks. Some of the younger ones didn't. I quickly understood that such a change in my appearance would be a signal to the others. As the only things I'd visibly done were patrol, guard, eat, and sleep, having marks would raise questions I couldn't answer.

Each shift thereafter, our time together started with lovemaking before we worked on my vocalizations. Troller taught me how my body worked as much as he taught me his language. When a vocalized concept eluded me, we used English to bridge the gap.

"The protectors all think I've lost my ability to vocalize because of my head injury. I think that's why I was assigned to you. There were whispers and concerns about your welfare, but they never say your name."

"They wouldn't, out of fear of being caught helping me. Halic has a lot of power. It's false power, and I need them to understand that."

"How, Troller?"

"By teaching you to vocalize clearly. And when the time is right, you'll convince as many as you can of the injustice happening."

"What happens to you? To Aisling?"

"I don't know. But hopefully, I can convince Aisling we need to make a better way for our people."

"Where are your adults?"

"Do you mean guardians?" He wrote the word "parents" in English, and I nodded. "I don't know. I haven't seen them, and I fear either Halic has banished them or they have stayed away out of fear. Halic doesn't need more leverage over me than he already has, and I'm afraid to ask anyone else in the pod."

I wrapped him in my arms. "Pete and Marcy's podling should be here. What's the word here for us that means our podling?"

He made a soft noise, and it reminded me of an old man grunt. I purred at him. "What does that mean?"

My purring didn't go unnoticed. Troller kissed me before he wrote "second guardians" on the ground. "Or close enough. I like the English word better. Also, you vocalized 'our podling,'" he clicked. "It's their podling," Troller indicated with a double click, and a small whistle. It made sense. The double click without the whistle was the 'them' pronoun. From what I could tell, podlings were gender neutral, and only adults had different pronouns.

"Close enough," I vocalized, and shrugged. As I detected the current shift that would bring the next shift of protectors, I kissed him like I had every night and left him with the same promise.

"I love you. I'll see you soon."

"I love you, Royce."

I took my place in the hall and shut the hatch behind me, and hated myself for it. I wanted us to leave, but I understood his need to see this through. If everything went according to Troller's plan, it would be over by the Yearend feast. We hoped that would be our chance to shift the tide.

A RELATIVE PROBLEM

TROLLER

I had a long time to think about what I could say to Aisling during her next visit. If we could have Royce assigned to her or someone Royce trusted, then we could talk.

Our luck came through when Phyris was assigned to Aisling. Royce trusted his peer. I only hoped that the protector he'd given the English name "Purple," which I corrected as soon as I discovered it, was as trustworthy.

When Aisling and Phyris arrived, Aisling was unusually quiet and reserved. I suspected something had happened. She glided to our table and set up the game.

"Are you alright?" I asked.

Her surprise was apparent at hearing my vocalizations. It quickly dissipated as she shook her head. If we'd been on land, I'm sure she would have cried. She glanced at Phyris and then back at me.

He approached carefully and put a hand on her shoulder. "Daako, her so-called mate, took her voice." Aisling reached up and squeezed Phyris' hand.

"Phyris, what do you know about Daako?" I asked, but I was afraid I already knew the answer.

"He treated Aisling well, but something changed when Halic took him on as his apprentice. He's become increasingly short with her and cruel. This happened because Aisling interrupted his spell practice. Others nearby corroborated the story."

I looked at Aisling. She nodded in agreement at Phyris's words. I felt sick. This turn of events explained why Halic hadn't visited me in some time. He had to be stopped.

"I'm going to tell you both everything that I know, and I hope you will help me. There isn't much time, and we need to be ready by the Yearend feast."

I explained who Royce was and why we trusted Phyris and Aisling. Of course, her being mute could be a ruse to trick Royce and me into giving ourselves away, but I hadn't seen that kind of forethought in Halic. I hoped Royce and I had put our trust in the right people.

"I knew I liked him. I mean, he's fairly awkward, but has a good heart. Are you teaching him?" Phyris queried.

I nodded. "It's been slow going, but Royce has learned a lot in a short amount of time."

"I can tell. Royce at least knows how to say his name now instead of calling himself councilor all the time."

I stifled a trill. If he had been born among my pod, it was likely he would have risen to councilor like I had. "He's a prince where he comes from, though he doesn't claim his heritage. He captain's a boat and is a natural leader, like his guardians." That reminded me. "Aisling, have you seen your guardians recently?" She responded by shaking her head no. "Do you remember the last time you saw them?" She considered and shook her head again.

Phyris vocalized, "Aisling's guardians have not returned to the pod caves since they promised her to Daako. Your guardians . . ." Phyris paused, and I was afraid of what he would vocalize. "Troller, when Halic came back to condemn you for going to the surface, your guardians were ostracized. They live in the outer areas. The pod was too afraid of Halic to protect them."

I was glad my guardians were alive, but it was bittersweet. If I could restore them to the pod, I would. They didn't deserve to be treated harshly for the choices I made. I keened softly and looked at my visitors. "Members of the pod need to risk the surface. They need to know they can shift without dying and understand that if they do it long enough, they might gain magic."

Phyris blinked, shock written across his features. Aisling looked paler, if that was possible.

"What you're suggesting is against everything the pods believe. You're here because you violated that tenet. And you would have others follow you?" Phyris queried.

"I suspect there are others that have already. Many saw me on the deck of Royce's boat the day Halic threatened to crush it with magic. They know I could breathe and walk." I played with a shell on the game board. "We have to find others that have tried or will try. If we can convince them to band together, work together to regain what we've lost, we can remove Halic and return to the surface. Then we can help others do the same."

Aisling nodded, but motioned to her throat. I wondered if my magic could fix or remove whatever Daako had done to her. Then maybe I could do the same for myself if Halic tried to silence me again.

"Stay still, Aisling. I'll attempt to help. If it works, you'll have to pretend to be silent until Halic or Daako gives your voice back, alright?" She nodded. I moved to her side and reached to touch her throat. At first nothing happened, then I concentrated and felt it—a blockage around her vocalizing cords. I massaged her throat with my hands, and the blockage slowly unraveled. "Try now."

"Troller?" Aisling clicked softly and smiled. "It worked."

"I'm glad. When my voice was stolen, I could tell something was wrong, but I didn't have the will to fix it." I looked between them again. "Are you with me?" They both nodded.

"Good. Do not deviate from your routines. If we can encourage enough of the pod to venture to the surface and possibly gain magic, Halic can't continue with his plans, whatever they are. The council wouldn't possibly punish the whole pod," I vocalized. "Phyris, help Royce communicate. Help him tell our story and explain how I gained magic."

As our visit ended, I felt hopeful that we might succeed. If we could find others and encourage them to be brave, there was a future for the pods—and the podlings that would not be born with fins, but feet instead.

As Aisling and Phyris prepared to swim away, I reached out and gently clasped her wrist. The movement and contact startled her, and she stopped to look at me. I came near her and opened my arms, like a guardian to a child. Her embrace was stiff at first, as if she was placating me. I held her closer and trilled and purred softly in reassurance and adoration. Her future mate had hurt her, and that was a trauma she would not soon forget.

She held me tighter then and shook with tremors I suspected were all her pent-up emotions. When she settled again, I let her go. She was brave. Much braver than I was at her age. "Whatever happens, I'll do everything I can to protect you, Aisling."

She gave a slight bow, and Phyris followed suit as I returned their acknowledgement. We were in agreement. I looked forward to telling Royce during his shift. I only hoped that all the risks we were taking would not make things worse.

When Royce arrived, he was agitated. He kissed me and we held each other for a time. When he calmed, a comfortable silence stretched between us. I found it ironic that everyone else around me was quiet while I had my voice.

"I'm worried. Phyris told me he knows, and he'd help me. Was that your doing?"

"Yes." I gave him a reassuring smile. "I am worried as well. Whatever happens, we have to tell the pod and let them decide."

"How do we stop Halic from hurting you or others? The magic he threatened my crew with was powerful. We don't know what else he can do. We don't know how long it will take others to develop magic. And even then, none of it will be as powerful as Halic's. He has too much of a head start."

I added more grave news to Royce's worries. "Halic taught Aisling's future mate to take her voice."

He was so agitated, he would have swum in circles if I hadn't grabbed hold of him.

"It's possible Daako isn't the only one he's training. What happens if the pod doesn't unite against Halic? What happens to us?" Royce fired off each question in a series of clicks and whistles, only missing a few tones in his rush to communicate.

I tried to reassure him with small caresses and fin movements. "Then we escape. We put as much distance between the pod and us as possible. We bring those with us that want to leave. Even I know there is only so much we can do, Royce. But we have to try. *I* have to try. I can't abandon my pod again."

Royce inhaled and exhaled with a soft whistle of agreement. "I told Galaina. She was grateful for the information." That was the waterfolk he had called Garden before I corrected him. I was grateful that she found Royce and took care of him. I hoped I could thank her myself one day. "Regardless of what happens, I'm here with you. We'll do this together."

We spent the rest of the time in each other's arms, hoping against hope that everything would be alright.

MARKING TIME

ROYCE

Phyris and I spread the story among the protectors, telling them about being able to shift, Troller's magic, the world above. What I couldn't vocalize, Phyris did. He reminded me of Pete, which was probably why I trusted him.

The first part of Troller's plan was to help anyone in the pod to the surface. The hope was that with subsequent trips, they would access their dormant magic.

Phyris and I escorted the latest group of waterfolk to a designated safe spot, near an outcropping we were sharing with some local seals, Phyris queried me, "Are you concerned about Troller's plan?" he asked as he left the water, and I stayed in the shallows near the outcropping.

"No. Troller wants to do the right thing and let them decide, not be duped into thinking they are here because surface dwellers will hunt them down the minute they breach the water."

"You said so yourself—you can't promise that won't happen."

"No, I can't. But it's different now. Surface dwellers have rules about sentient life, and we all live together with much less conflict than before. I can barely use magic, and what I can use is made for humans that don't have access to it or don't have magic themselves. People have shelter, don't starve, and most places are safe.

"There are likely things I don't know, and being a human, well, it's certainly a kind of privilege. But all I can do is share my experiences and help with the newness of surface life as much as I can."

Phyris nodded. "Then we will maintain faith that the pod will follow the right leader and choose wisely. Troller will have his chance to speak at the Yearend feast as the pod's council member. Halic won't go so far against tradition to not allow it."

"Why haven't they replaced Troller on the council?" I wondered about it since Troller wasn't allowed to perform many of his duties, only the ceremonial ones. Not that I knew anything about what a council member did for the pod, other than representing them.

"I imagine it's tied in with his punishment. Halic has been our pod's acting council member since Troller supposedly died by going to the surface. Once he returned, Troller wouldn't hand his position over to Aisling, and Halic's story is unraveling. The other council members are unsure of what to do. Halic has made a strong case for keeping Troller confined to make sure he can't steal Halic's magic too. Many trusted Halic as an elder of the pods because of his magic. Troller is the only one who openly defied Halic."

There were rumors among the protectors that the council was reconsidering Troller's confinement. While they acknowledged he was a councilor and should have known better, the news of how he used his magic to help so many had begun to sway the council.

"Hasn't anyone attempted the surface before this?" I queried.

"Maybe. But for most of us, there are enough dangers in the surrounding waters. Why should we court more?"

Phyris' logic made sense. The council was being cautious. None of the protectors nor Galaina, who had a ranking in the pod of elder guardian, understood why the council had confined Troller. The action was odd to them, even though some now knew the truth. All of it spoke of a species with long-held traditions and ideas that were deeply ingrained in their lives. Changing that would take time. Troller and I hoped our stories helped, but I continued to wonder if it would be enough.

After months of venturing to the surface and shifting, Troller's hope was fulfilled, and they began manifesting magic. Some were healers; others could do simple things, like glamour, which allowed the waterfolk to change small parts of their appearance and even seem to disappear. One waterfolk shifted into other kinds of aquatic species—a turtle, then a dolphin, and even an octopus. When they figured out their proper form again, they were elated.

Troller and I had been gone for nearly a year, as we reckoned time by the birthing cycles and the feasts. My parents, Pete and

Marcy, the crew, none of them would know anything about what happened to us. Once Troller's pod was safe, I hoped we could find a way to tell them we were safe.

While we clandestinely helped the pod, Halic pressured Troller to change his story. Halic knew he was losing control of the council, but didn't know why. We were lucky he never recognized me or noticed my marks on Troller during these visitations. He always kept a loyal protector near him and the reed hatch between him and Troller.

Our quiet opposition grew. By the time the Yearend feast approached, nearly half the pod had ventured to the surface. A third of those continued to leave the water.

I told stories about the surface, preparing them for the time waterfolk no longer lived in isolation.

Moment of Truth

Royce

On the day of the Yearend feast, we swam down the passage toward Aisling's room. Our plan was to have Phyris protect Aisling and swim her out of danger if necessary. I would defend Troller. Even though I wasn't assigned to him for the feast, my presence wouldn't cause much of a stir as most of the pod was expected to be there, including Halic.

We were only a short passageway from Aisling's room when we heard a shrill noise. Phyris and I moved quickly and arrived at the room as one of Aisling's protectors swam out of her dwelling.

"What happened?" I queried.

"Daako attacked Aisling. I'm retrieving a healer," Aisling's protector vocalized.

I entered her room. Another protector was vocalizing with Phyris when I went inside.

"Aisling, are you alright?" I did not know her well, but Troller and Phyris trusted her, and I trusted them.

The girl swam toward me and wrapped her arms around my neck. "Royce! Daako is not himself. He kept saying these awful things. That we would rule the pods, and our podlings would be powerful, and that I was lying to him about not being ready to mate yet. He tried to pin me, so I hit him in the nose."

I held her as she shook from the stress and violence of what happened. The pods taught children to defend themselves from predators, like sharks. I doubt Aisling thought she'd have to protect herself from someone who was supposed to care about her.

"You're alright now. Another protector went to find a healer." Aisling nodded. Another waterfolk came inside carrying woven reed bindings. I watched as he looped them around Daako's neck and wrist, then pulled them tight. Phyris stayed next to Daako's prone form, which floated in the center of the room. Aisling and I maintained our position near where I had found her.

"Are you alright, Aisling?" Phyris queried.

She nodded. "What do we do now?"

I wondered about that myself. "The feast will start soon. I need to find Troller."

Daako blinked a few times, then opened his eyes. He didn't fight the bindings. Instead, he shifted and vomited. Phyris whistled for cleaning fish, which quickly swam in from various parts of the room and gobbled up the mess.

We watched as Daako wiped his mouth and looked up at us, then at his bindings. "Where am I?" he queried.

"You're in Aisling's room. Do you not remember coming here to meet her for the Yearend feast?" I explained.

"No. Truly, I do not. The last thing I remember is attending Elder Councilor Halic in his chamber for lessons," Daako vocalized.

"When was that?" Phyris had a tone of uncertainty in his query, given what happened.

The youngling looked distraught. He reached up and touched the braids in his hair. I had learned that younglings who courted each other would make braids of a specific pattern to show they were involved. The more braids of the same pattern, the longer the courtship. Daako looked at Aisling. She turned her head to his silent plea, showing her braids. I noticed the patterns matched as well. He looked at all of us, then vocalized. "I remember the Midyear feast, and swimming with Aisling. Halic bid me to stay here in the pod caves, so I did. My first lesson was not long after that. Maybe six current shifts? I don't remember the lesson. But clearly, much time has passed."

Daako and Aisling exchanged a look, and she ducked her head into my arm. The Gulf had two tides a day, so three days, give or take. If that's all he remembered, then Daako had been in Halic's control for months.

"Sing, please, what happened?" Daako vocalized. The affectionate name was not lost on anyone in the room.

I looked at Phyris, then we glanced at Aisling.

"You haven't called me that since you came to the pod caves," Aisling cooed.

Daako looked at all of us, and I could see his fear. Not only for himself, but Aisling as well. I wondered what Halic had done to the youngling.

"How long have I been here?" Daako whistled as he held out his bound wrists. The panic in his vocalizations made us all flinch. "Please, what's happened?"

Phyris was not gentle. "It's the day of the Yearend feast. You've taken Aisling's voice several times, and earlier, you tried to harm her. She defended herself."

Daako shook his head. "That can't be. I wouldn't do that. Never!" The odd keening with the low-toned purr caused Aisling to move from the safety of my arms toward Daako. She circled around him, then pulled him into her arms. He shook with emotion, and we watched as they made soft noises to each other and touched their braids.

I moved closer to Phyris. "Is Halic powerful enough to control someone's mind?" I queried.

"Possible. Maybe a kind of mesmerism. Instructions put in the youngling's brain. We have stories about power like that named Siren's Call. It was to lure surface dwellers to their deaths or control them to fight with each other," Phyris explained.

I looked at Phyris and made a whistle of surprise.

"Yes, agreed. I thought they were stories, too. But this doesn't seem like a story any longer."

Aisling freed Daako from his bindings. They kissed chastely and turned toward us. "Halic will pay for this," Aisling vocalized in a low noted call.

"First, we need to meet Troller at the feast, or we might miss the chance. I felt the current shift a little while ago," I responded. We organized ourselves and headed toward the feast hall. A healer met us and swam alongside Daako to ensure he was swimming correctly. The youngling looked determined, even though his nose looked bruised.

As we moved down the passage, I tried to calm the young pair. "Daako, how did you and Aisling meet?" I vocalized.

"Halic brought Aisling with him when he came to my home and asked my guardians to see me. He vocalized with my guardians and eventually offered to mentor me in his ways. Aisling and I spent time together as we swam back here to her pod."

I looked at Phyris. "That seems fairly random, doesn't it?"

"I understand very little about Halic's motivations other than power," Phyris clicked. "There are many strange things in the water. Take yourself, for instance."

"I'm not from here, that's certain, but how is that strange?"

"There are very few of us that have facial hair. We know you're a surface dweller now, but before, we thought it might be why Councilor Troller favored you," Phyris vocalized.

"Huh." I turned to Phyris as our group went into the feasting hall. "How would anyone know?" I didn't have any marks. Troller made sure of that. Something I wanted to correct soon.

Phyris leaned in and clicked softly. "Councilor Troller always had fresh marks after your shift, and his face was bright, as if scrubbed clean."

"Does no one realize how observant protectors are?" I felt like I was blushing, but had no idea if that was visible or not.

"They often don't. Which is why we know so much about the community." Phyris smiled.

We went into the feast hall. As we positioned ourselves, I noticed two things.

"Phyris, where are Halic and Troller?" I queried. Phyris looked around.

"Halic and Troller should be here. They're supposed to be here."

I had a horrible feeling. I swam out of the feast hall back toward the room where Troller was kept. My cries of anguish echoed along the hall when I saw fellow protectors floating outside of Troller's room like stunned fish. The hatch was open, and Troller... Troller was gone.

TEST OF WILLS

TROLLER

"Troller, damn your gills, open your eyes," Halic demanded in loud tones and clicks. It echoed in the space we were in, sounding too large. It was much larger than the room they had held me in.

"You ruined everything. We could have worked together, but you had to subvert everything, and now all is lost."

Halic was raving. I finally opened my eyes to see that my hands were bound by reeds with a loop around my neck. Was this it? Would Halic kill me? Had he discovered what Royce and the others were doing?

"I've spent so long, a lifetime keeping the pods safe. Why did you follow me, Troller? Why did you come to the surface that day?"

I shook my head. I didn't know what to vocalize. Curiosity and concern seemed an inadequate excuse, considering everything that followed.

"So many hatchlings." Halic turned and pressed a glowing object into the wall. It lit the cavern we were in. But it wasn't just a cavern; it was a hatchery. Hundreds of eggs lined the walls. They glowed with life, though the beats were long and steady. "These are all the hatchlings I've rescued over the years. The ones that wouldn't have survived below the surface. I took them from the fields and stored them here, let the birth guardians think predators had taken their eggs. It was kinder."

He swam toward me and grabbed the reed rope. His nose nearly touched mine. "Cycles upon cycles, trying to discover how to make them shift to a safe form, and you appear with a magic that can do it, with just a thought." He pushed me away, and I struggled to orient myself to the room. "All I've ever been able to do is mend wounds. The barest of healing magic. But you can remove scars and wounds as if they never happened." He let out a low, annoyed whistle. "How did you learn this magic?" His clicks were harsh.

"I've given you the same answer every time," I vocalized. "I went to the surface and eventually it manifested."

"No, you have to be lying."

I tried to remain calm. It wasn't only my life in danger. There were hundreds of eggs in the chamber. "Why? You went to the surface. You developed your magic there. Why am I lying?"

"Because," Halic moved and shoved something into a piece of rock that protruded from the floor, "I learned what I know from him."

An image appeared over the rock. A young man with brown hair and a freckled rosy complexion, but irises as black as mine in my surface form. It looked like Halic had activated a holo device.

"His name was Logan." Halic stared at the man in the image. "He was one of us, but lived on the surface. He saved us from the surface dwellers. I found his study and read his notes. Used his devices."

He moved to look at me. "I tried to use his knowledge to help the hatchlings without taking them to the surface. But Logan only wrote of other things and masking our auras to protect us from being discovered by the surface dwellers. While I found nothing significant, I learned about harnessing moon power." He reached for something in his white hair, and only then did I realize he'd woven an amulet into it. I wondered if he had more hidden in his many braids.

"It lets me control water, and sometimes even the tides."

The wave that almost destroyed Royce's boat and the crew. "Let us help you, Halic. The pod deserves to know these things. We can help you."

"It's not safe. It won't ever be safe." Halic narrowed his eyes. "They hunted Logan down. He hid his study so the surface dwellers couldn't find it. We can't go back to the surface."

"Halic, it's too late. Many have returned to the surface. Some even developed magic. I lived there for almost a year, and I returned unharmed. It's possible," I pointed at all the hatchlings, "for these eggs to be hatched somewhere protected, where they can shift naturally. Waterfolk don't have to hide any longer."

"No! That's not our way!"

"It used to be. At some point, a long time ago, it used to be. We can restore . . ."

"Lies from the surface dwellers . . . LIES!" He swam at me, and I couldn't maneuver fast enough to dodge him. I hit my head as he slammed me against the rough wall. The impact caused me to black out for a few moments. When I woke, Halic was gone.

Now that I wasn't afraid for my life or the eggs, I took in my surroundings. The chamber was beautiful. It must have been built specifically to protect our hatchlings, but somehow the pods lost the knowledge of this place.

I swam until I found an opening. There was barely any light, and what was there had a dull bioluminescence. I swam into another opening and kept going until I found myself in another chamber that looked much like the rooms in the pod caves. However, this one had another passage that was barely large enough for one individual's width. Some protectors would have had a difficult time passing through it. When I emerged, it was in an alcove that was partially blocked by an old cave-in. Whether it was on purpose or by accident, someone had hidden this passage, and Halic had found it.

As I freed myself from the blocked alcove, I heard my name and Halic's echoing along the currents. I called back. I heard more calls and clicks. Then I heard Royce's vocalizations calling for me.

When Royce reached me, he removed my bonds and held me tight. I clung to him. If it was in my power, I'd never be separated from him again.

YEAREND FEAST

ROYCE

No one could find Halic. We could only hope that he didn't show himself at the Yearend feast. It would be much easier to help Troller's pod find its way back to the surface without Halic's opposition. We had support from many who broke with tradition and went to the surface, walked on beaches, and developed magic. I hoped they sided with Troller and Aisling. I wanted to believe that we would succeed.

In my eyes, Troller was never weak, though he thought he was because of how he'd left things with his pod. Even though they brought him back against his will, to see him work hard for his pod and fight for them to have a better life was inspiring. I often wondered what my parents would think about it, and I hoped we could tell them one day.

The pang of homesickness was genuine as I looked around. My parents would host a similar party for charity or some such event during the winter holidays. It was strange to realize that I hadn't spoken to them for a year or more.

A low bell tone rang out in the feast hall, drawing everyone's attention. Troller gave a subtle motion with his fluke, which sent him above the flat surface where all the food was placed. He was poised with a regal look about him that would rival any royal court on the surface. From the way his hair was adorned and woven, to the woven reeds that flowed from his arms like princely vestments. He held his hands in front of him, clasped loosely, in the way an opera singer would.

It was an apt comparison considering what was at stake and what Troller needed to vocalize to convince people of their circumstance and what should be done about it.

"We have gathered at this year's end to celebrate and bless the past year while we welcome a new one. However, I cannot do so. There is so much which you have been denied, and so much I wish to help us change." The feast hall was quiet. Everyone looked at Troller and waited.

"We were deceived. As your councilor, I took it upon myself to discover why Halic had such magic when others did not. His magic comes from a special place on the surface. He's learned much since he discovered it.

"My magic also comes from the surface, but I did not learn it. It manifested during my time above the water. I've helped many here as proof that magic does not have to be harmful. Others here can share."

The silence in the room was like old seaweed on my tongue. I feared no one would be brave enough to come forward. Phyris moved and for a moment, I thought it was to protect me. Instead, he vocalized his story.

"I've been to the surface many times. I do not have magic like Troller, but each time I went to the surface, I grew stronger.

I'm able to move large rocks without effort. Swim long distances without tiring. My strength is more than it was before."

After Phyris spoke, another came forward, then another. The secret rebellion came out into the open as those that had ventured to the surface over several months told their stories.

There were angry clicks, but with each new story, the clicks died away. When over half the pod, including several elders, had told their stories, those that were angry quieted. Then the angry turned into the curious. Their queries came quickly, and Troller held up a hand to forestall them.

"First, I want to assure you I'll try very hard to answer each question and each concern you have. I've never stopped being your councilor, and I hope you will trust me to take up my duties again." There were clicks of agreement, and Troller lowered his hand.

"When Halic is found, he will receive the justice he deserves. Justice, he did not grant me when I was returned here against my will." The vocalizations varied, but many sounded upset that Halic had fled. Troller lifted his arms and whistled to gain everyone's attention again.

"As for surface dwellers . . ." He turned to look for me and held out his hand. I swam to him and took it. "Royce comes from the surface. He and those he calls family and friends are some of the most wonderful individuals I've had the pleasure of meeting. Most of you in the community know Royce. You know what he's contributed here since he arrived. I cannot vouch for everyone above the waterline, but I can say this: we don't have to hide here, isolated and separate from the world above. There are things we can experience and learn, and there are things they can learn from us as well."

Troller looked at me, and I was smiling from ear to ear. He was free, and we would be free to be with each other now that the truth was out in the open. "Furthermore, I submit myself for judgment to the council. I have incited unrest among our community and encouraged many to break with tradition. I implore you to hold me accountable for their actions once you reach a decision about whether or not we should return to the surface."

Other councilors approached. One with raven hair shot through with white and gray vocalized first. "Councilor Troller, we accept your willingness to be judged." A blue flame appeared in her hand. "But then, I'm afraid the entire council would need to similarly be judged."

I was shocked. The councilor wasn't among those Phyris and I had escorted to the surface. It means someone must have told them and they decided to see for themselves. That's the only explanation I could think of. Otherwise, how did the councilor have magic?

Troller smiled. "Councilor Ossen. Thank you for your vote of confidence. When the council convenes next, I implore that Councilor Halic is treated with mercy when he is found."

"Why, Councilor Troller?" Ossen vocalized.

"I won't make the same mistakes he did. It would make me no better than him."

Ossen nodded and clicked. "I understand your wisdom and lenience. We will see that the punishment is merciful."

The room was quiet for a moment, then Troller called out to the gathered waterfolk, "There is plenty for all. Please enjoy the feast. We celebrate a new age, and we should enjoy it properly."

"Cheers for Councilor Troller!" Phyris sang.

The pod responded, and their sound resonated around the room. It wasn't like the cheering you'd hear at sports events or celebrations back home. It was a tone of pure happiness and joy. I couldn't help myself at that moment, and I moved toward Troller to give him a very thorough kiss. When we stopped, members of the community surged forward to congratulate us and offer us small tokens.

"Why are they giving us things?" I queried softly to Troller when there was a slight break in the wave of waterfolk greeting us. Troller smiled.

"How should I explain this, my love?"

"Simply, please," I vocalized.

"To publicly show affection means to declare someone your mate," Troller explained.

"Wait, you mean we're married?"

Troller gave me a slight nod.

"Are you alright with that?" I was worried, but not for myself. I was more than alright with being married to Troller, but I hadn't expected to make that choice alone.

Troller swam closer. "Do you think I would have let you kiss me if I weren't?" He smiled, and I trilled and purred.

"I love you, Troller."

"I feel the same, my love," Troller vocalized, and gave me another kiss.

THE LOST

Troller

Royce and I held hands in the open in front of our pod for the first time. With Royce by my side, anything seemed possible. It was exhilarating how much better I felt now that we could be together, with everyone watching and no fear of reprisal from Halic.

The feast slowly ended. We'd won. I was elated, but also concerned. The pod would need to work together to overcome the lies and fear. It would take time, but I was sure they would band together and find solutions.

As we swam out of the feasting hall together, Royce smiled at me. "You know, the protectors knew about us the whole time."

"They did?" That was surprising.

"It seems they noticed your marks. And your face."

"Oh." I must have looked silly because Royce trilled, then he softly hummed to me.

"You didn't have marks before I gave them to you," Royce vocalized softly.

I nodded in agreement. Royce came closer, then swam us to a small alcove.

"Why didn't you tell me?" His vocalization was full of concern and desire. I thought back to the first time we had coupled when I was in my surface form. I'd been driven by instinct. I wasn't completely innocent, but I hadn't taken a lover until then.

"The first time we were together, we marked each other with something no one could see, but only we could feel. When we came together here for the first time, your marks were a physical manifestation of everything I feel for you. It's how I reminded myself that you were here and you were real. And every time you renewed them, I vibrated with the joy I felt at seeing and feeling them on my body."

I pressed myself against him, pushing him against the alcove wall. I used my fluke with quick swishes of my fins to keep him pinned in place. I put my hands on either side of his head and looked into his eyes, so similar to mine now. "You are my first Royce and you will be my last. My mate. And later in my chamber, I very much plan on giving you marks no one will miss."

Royce's eyes were wide, his heartbeat fast against my chest. It thrilled me. His hand rose to trace his thumb over my jawline, then it wrapped around the back of my neck in a comforting hold as he looked at me.

"As you wish, my love." He encouraged me forward, and I pressed my lips into his, parting them to let us kiss deeply. His arms wrapped around me, and I stopped keeping us in place.

The feeling of slowly turning and kissing as we swam in the alcove proved headier than I realized. We might not make it until we returned to my chamber after all. My arms tightened around

Royce as my hands slipped to his waist and hips. I felt Royce do the same and the pricks of his claws preparing to break my flesh when a soft vocalization surprised us.

I turned to look at Phyris, Aisling, and Daako. Royce hid his face in my neck. Surface dwellers were embarrassed so easily.

"Can I help you, Phyris?" I queried, my tone even despite the circumstances.

"Halic has fled the caves. Protectors are still looking for him, but with no way of knowing where he'd gone or if he'd return, we have little hope of finding him," he vocalized. "However, you had mentioned wanting to look at the rooms Halic took you to after the feast. Would you prefer we wait for a current shift or two?"

Phyris glanced between Royce and me with an apologetic look that matched the tone of his query. I shook my head. "No, best to do it now so others can help. Could you ask Councilor Ossen to join us?" She was the next elder council member after Halic.

Phyris nodded, and when he returned with the councilor, I led our group to where I exited the network of rooms and passages that led to the hatchery. "It's not a hard path to follow."

Phyris twitched his fins and moved forward. "I'll go first to make sure Halic did not retreat to this location." Daako followed, then Aisling, and Councilor Ossen. Royce stayed with me.

The sight of the entrance made my throat constrict. It wasn't fear exactly, but the possibility that I would be trapped again once I entered the passage. A greater fear took its place as I imagined Royce trapped. I shook my head and tried to vocalize, but nothing came out.

Royce held me while I calmed myself. I laid my head on Royce's shoulder while my emotions vibrated through my body. What if it had been an elaborate trap? Phyris was Royce's friend. Aisling and Daako were innocent. It would be unacceptable if we lost them.

Royce held me tighter, and I felt him shiver in response. "It's alright, Troller. You need not return to this place if it bothers you."

"When my pod first brought me back," I vocalized softly, "they kept me in a place no larger than that passage."

Royce held me tighter. "I should have tried harder," he keened. "I should have found you sooner."

"You found me, Royce. That's everything that matters. You found me, and we're together."

I felt his hand caress my head and hair, then his lips kissed my temple. "I will always find you, Troller, always."

"I will do the same, my love."

I gathered my courage. It would help if I could explain what I found. I went through the entrance and glanced behind me. Royce followed and encouraged me with his vocalizations. "Keep going, my love. I'm here."

I met the rest of our group in the old room that had the passage to the hatchery. The silt was stirred up from so many small fin movements. It gave the room an ominous feeling with its murky opacity.

"What I'd like to show you is through the next passage. I believe Halic found this place but kept it a secret from everyone." Before I lost my nerve, I moved into the passage. Royce was behind me, and everyone else followed.

When we all arrived in the hatchery, I moved to the same platform Halic had used to show me Logan's face. The chamber was still lit with one of the crystals.

Daako looked at me with excitement. Aisling swam in small circles, peering into one hole, then another. "There are eggs here," clicked Aisling.

"Why?" Councilor Ossen queried, obviously curious about what Halic was doing with so many of the pod's eggs.

"They are in some kind of stasis," Daako vocalized.

Now that I wasn't in fear for my life or the hatchlings, I could appreciate the hatchery and its ingenuity. It held a latticework of chambers that reminded me of a beehive.

"Daako is correct. Halic stole these eggs from the birthing grounds and put them into stasis. He hoped, so he told me, to learn how to shift them to their water form. These hatchlings are in their surface form in one way or another. There are years upon years' worth of eggs kept here in stasis to save them."

"This is why you asked for mercy," Ossen vocalized.

I nodded. "While some things he did caused irreparable harm to the pod, his original goal was to save these hatchlings from dying at birth because they were born under water instead of on the surface, like the generations of old."

Daako touched the platform next to me, and it came to life. Logan's face once again filled the space above the platform's surface.

"I believe this is a knowledge center. There are other crystals, but this is the one Halic showed me of Logan. Halic vocalized that Logan helped conceal the magical auras of waterfolk to protect them from surface dwellers."

"The concealment worked so well that we forgot part of ourselves in the process. There have been generations that knew nothing of Logan and his achievements." Ossen's vocalizations held a note of sorrow. I felt the same way.

The soft glow from the knowledge center put the chamber into relief. There were more small chambers all along the walls.

Daako picked up another crystal and placed it into the pedestal. It came to life, then sound came out of it.

"My home is the sea,
My love lives on land with me.
We sail the waters with carefree hearts,
With gills and lungs, we sing as one.
May our joy of the waves keep us together,
May we never part."

The story that followed enraptured our group, hearing our history sung to us by someone from the distant past. A recorded history that wasn't supposed to have existed.

Aisling vocalized after the storyteller's song ended. "Some chambers don't have eggs; they have crystals. There are hundreds of crystals here. Several lifetimes' worth of work."

I looked again at the structure that played the vocalizations. "This looks familiar. Does it look familiar to anyone else?"

Aisling swished her tail in excitement. "The feast hall!"

"Yes. Shall we try it?" I queried.

They all nodded. I took another crystal with us. As we went through the passage, one by one, the small amount of information we'd heard floated through my mind. At some point, the pods had been a full-fledged society that walked on land and swam in the sea.

I cleared the tunnel and didn't wait for Royce to follow me through the passage from the hidden room and the blocked alcove. Once in the main passage, we swam to the main feast hall. In the center of the hall, the protrusion from the floor was easy to recognize. It often held food, but there were carved slots in it. No one had wondered why those slots were there, not even me.

I approached the protrusion and inserted the crystal into one of the slots. It lit up and immediately played the historical record in the crystal.

Not only had the chamber kept the eggs, it also kept our histories. Even if Halic hadn't started it, he continued to keep everyone in the dark. How had he found the chamber to begin with?

When the crystal hit a resonating point, the walls of the feast hall lit up, and everyone gasped as we saw the images projected along with the vocalizations. We watched and listened. It spoke of a time when waterfolk freely came and went from the sea. We were fishers and traders. We also helped rescue ships and find wrecks for a fee.

"Have you ever seen anything like this?" Royce queried.

"No, and neither has anyone else. Probably for generations." I looked at the group gathered around me and the images on the walls. "That changes now. We will learn who we are, and they will decide what to do next." Royce took my hand as we watched the past dance and sing.

LOVER'S MARKS

ROYCE

We learned a lot from the singing crystals.

Around the time that surface dwellers ventured across the Atlantic, different pods did too. Surface dwellers and waterfolk clashed when it was discovered that they had come with the boats. The waterfolk worked to protect the indigenous to the area, and the European slaughtered them both, trying to gain the new magic and land.

Some surface dwellers collaborated with them instead of fighting. They set up ports, and the waterfolk protected the seaports and the indigenous as best they could. When several ports were lost to pirates and invading forces, they accused the waterfolk of working with them. If caught by surface dwellers from either side, they were executed.

It was gruesome. Shortly after that, the waterfolk retreated to the sea. One of the few safe places they had. They used beaches for hatchlings until they became too populated by surface dwellers to safely hatch the eggs.

"This was after the Magical Species Pact." I noted as we watched another of Troller's ancestors sing about their history. The pact changed access to magic in most of Europe and hadn't protected anyone in the Americas. Once a different source of magic was found, they came here hoping to claim it. No wonder Europeans flocked to the Americas.

"What's this law you speak of, Royce?" Troller looked between me and the current lesson playing on the walls in the dining hall.

"I'll explain later."

Troller tilted his head in a curiosity and gave me a nod.

The lesson continued with stories of the waterfolk thriving under the sea. The storyteller ended their song, hoping waterfolk might rejoin the surface dwellers again.

Troller took my hand. He looked tired. After all that had happened, it didn't surprise me. I felt like I'd been dragged by a boat myself.

"Phyris, could you take word to the councilors that we should meet in two current shifts' time to discuss what we've found?" Troller vocalized.

He nodded. "It would be my pleasure," Phyris vocalized, and left the rest of us in the feast hall.

Troller turned to Aisling. "Let's hope for no more excitement before the next current shift. You and Daako should stay together. Let the protectors safeguard you both for the evening. Alright?"

Aisling agreed. She and Daako joined hands, encouraged by Troller's concern. "Until the next current, Councilor Troller," she vocalized. Troller nodded, and we watched them leave the hall. Two protectors gracefully dove behind the pair and left us mostly to ourselves. I noticed six other protectors spaced around the feast hall, vigilant and ever-watching. They would take news of the find back to the other protectors. For now, they watched us, likely asked to keep an eye on their restored councilor.

"Would you like to rest, Troller?" I queried.

His lips curved into a subtle smile before he answered. "Not exactly, but I want to find a place more suited."

I offered my hand, and he took it. "Lead the way."

We swam out of the feast hall, then into the passages and out of the rear entrance of the pod caves, which the protectors often used to return to their cave. A pair followed us, swimming several meters back.

We arrived at a small cave structure on the side of a drop-off at the edge of the pod. I marveled at the view. The opening was modest; the inside was overgrown with moss, and there were objects everywhere. Some recognizable, some otherwise. I swam over to what looked like several small ledges carved into the stone.

"Is this a light?" I picked up what looked like a waterproof dive light and clicked it on. Amazed that it still had power, it lit up the ceiling. The light danced across many colorful rocks plastered in with the moss. "Where are we?"

"This used to be mine. When I became an adult, my guardians brought me here. It belonged to someone in our family. That person was fascinated with surface dweller things, and I continued their collection. The last time I was here was before I met you."

"It's cozy."

Troller trilled at my description. "Yes, cozy and private. It's not spelled for quiet, but it will do."

"Oh," I vocalized as he swam up to me. I shut off the light and plunged us into a bioluminated darkness.

I let Troller take the lead. Our kisses were intense. Troller swam us into a wall and pinned me there, using his fins to keep us pressed together. I wrapped my arms around him, and he continued lavishing me with kisses that teased with our dexterous tongues. The sharp teeth were not a deterrent.

Troller paused a moment with his hand pressed to my chest. His other hand went for my genital pouch. I felt two of his fingers press into me and caress my hardness. I closed my eyes, letting the sensations drift over me. Everything in the water was erotic, to some extent. The minutest flow of water along my back and hips, the swirls from Troller's hip fins, the nearly synchronized swishes of our flukes.

"Troller," I vocalized softly. When I felt the temperature change, I opened my eyes to see Troller pull my cock from my pouch. It was bright red and stiff from his handling. It looked different from my human one, but no less impressive. I must have made a noise because Troller agreed.

"You are impressive. I wonder what it would be like to make love to you in my surface form while you are in this one," Troller teased as he adjusted his position. He let go of me for a moment and brought my arm around his waist. He flicked his hip fins and put himself perpendicular to my hips, so his head was near my groin.

"You said I don't have to be quiet, yes?" I queried.

"No, not here, my love. Not here." His lips wrapped around me, and I cried out in a trilling moan that echoed along the walls. My sensitivity was so different. When we'd tried this before, I had made too much noise. Troller had to stop before he'd barely started. I couldn't help how sensitive I was outside my pouch or Troller's.

We floated up to the ceiling as I held onto Troller. I put a hand up to brace myself from smacking my head. Troller seemed unphased by the drift from our original position. "You have to stop," I indicated with a groaned vocalization. "I'm close, Troller."

His head pulled away from me, and the mix of warmth from Troller's mouth and the cool water that slid past my dick made a moan escape my throat. Troller maneuvered again to bring us face to face.

He took out his own cock and slid it against mine. It seemed more lewd somehow, and the gentle friction almost did me in. Before I could think about it, Troller reached between us and lined us up. I tried to stay with him as he pushed the head of himself into my pouch and then pushed the head of my cock into his. The way his pouch hugged my tip while his filled mine was already mind-blowing. I hoped it was the same for him. I barely had time to see the erotic image of our mutual penetration before Troller's hands moved to my hips and, in one swift motion, slammed us both fully inside each other.

"Oh, shit."

Troller trilled and purred a little. I felt his nails prick at the scales on my hips. He kissed me softly and then vocalized. "If I do this right, you shouldn't feel it until after. And it might bother you at first, but . . ."

"Troller," I vocalized. "I've waited long enough. I want your marks. Please."

He gave me a small nod and moved slightly. It was a completely distinct feeling from what we'd mostly done before, which I suspected was to keep me from being marked. Slight movements between us had me vocalizing, and we both instinctively grasped onto each other's hips, breaking the skin. A sensation, which wasn't quite pain, but something akin to it, drove me. It drove us both. Small swirls of water and moss floated around us as our hips made small movements, and we dug furrows into each other.

"Troller..." I captured his lips with mine, then just as I came into him, I bit his lip.

"Royce," he moaned and vocalized. His hands moved from my hips to just under my arms and over my back. I felt the prick of his claws, and when he finally came, he drew his hands across my back. I vocalized something and clawed his back as I came again. We stayed like that for a time until we both settled against the ceiling of the room like dead fish.

I had noticed all the chambers had moss on the ceilings, even the shelf I slept on back in the protector cave. The moss absorbed our spend and blood. I didn't remember falling asleep, but I had Troller in my arms, so nothing else mattered.

When I opened my eyes, two protectors were below us, looking up. I closed my eyes and opened them again, hoping I was seeing things. Instead, I identified Mareef and Dena, who I had been on several patrols with during my time here.

"Sorry to disturb your sleep. We've had news from the pod caves."

"What news?" Troller queried. His vocalizations were soft and sleepy. I hadn't realized he was awake. His back was to me, pressed to my chest, and his hips were pressed into my groin.

"The pod has been searched, but we suspect Halic went into deep water. Several protectors have not checked in. We believe he might have enlisted their help." Dena's hip fins swished in an agitated fashion as she relayed the information. "The council also sent us to ask you to attend a meeting about the hatchery you found."

Troller nodded. "We will come with you." They nodded and left the dwelling. He moved away from me, and I saw that Troller's back had eight furrows down it, along with five gouges on each hip. My hips had similar markings. However, the ones on my back were crossed, like an X.

"How do you feel?" he queried.

"Amazing and tired," I vocalized. "I hoped they would find Halic."

"Well, once word spreads of his duplicity to other pods, he won't be able to shelter anywhere."

"Maybe we'll be lucky enough a shark finds him," I trilled.

"Royce!" The sharp tone in my name made me trill.

"Only speaking my mind. We should start moving before our protectors return."

We swam back to the caves and received looks that were a mixture of impressed, jealous, and congratulatory from individuals who swam by. The protectors led us into the same feast hall. There was another crystal playing, and this time it was about the podlings.

INHERITANCE

TROLLER

When Royce and I entered the room, the only thing I heard was the tones of another storyteller describing the previously hidden cavern. From their description, the whole pod and even neighboring pods used the hatchery to protect their young from predators.

They described magical attributes often displayed in their eggs before they hatched.

"When exposed to sunlight, eggs will illuminate to show the potential magical properties the hatchlings might have after they emerge. This tradition of sunbathing eggs helps guardians plan for the podling's future education. The following colors or magical auras relate to each magical practice. Green auras usually indicate healing, transfiguration, and fertility. Red auras indicate..."

"Did the storyteller say what I think they said?" Royce queried.

"I believe so." I was excited, and angry. If we were all born with magic, then our fear had nearly destroyed our culture and tradition. Halic's discovery could have changed that, but instead, he used it to his advantage and created more fear instead of understanding.

I made a hand motion that caught Daako's attention, and he made another to pause the auditory information. "Were you able to find anything about the hatchlings in stasis?"

He shook his head. "No, not yet."

Daako glanced at the knowledge platform, then at me. "I don't understand how Halic taught me magic even though I haven't ventured to the surface, nor do I remember any specific lessons."

"Are you sure of that?" Royce queried. "You were under his control for a time. He could have taken you to the surface, and you might not have known." Daako let out a slight clicking noise of distress. It hadn't occurred to him how deeply Halic might have betrayed him.

I reached out and touched Daako's shoulder. "It's alright. We'll work through this together. You are not alone." Daako clicked his agreement. "Could you continue the recording for us, please, Daako?" I noticed Aisling nearby. After restarting the recording, she took his hand as they listened and watched it side by side.

The storyteller continued and mentioned that white auras meant the podling would have more innate magic and often abilities cultivated around physical magic. A waterfolk named Ulrich, with this physical magic, made the cavern where the eggs were in stasis. It was originally meant to keep them safe from predators. It seems the stasis spells were designed as an option, not something for long-term use. They also created the system that allowed people to record vocalizations and images into crystals.

Individuals with purple auras had less innate magic but often had more physical abilities, such as keen sight, hearing, strength, or endurance. These individuals sometimes became the natural protectors of the pod and helped nurture and defend the pod from dangers. It was discovered, much by accident, that they could also use their blood as a powerful catalyst for magic.

"Those with a brown aura . . ." the storyteller sang.

"Brown? How many auras and types of abilities are there?" Phyris vocalized.

". . . are rare gifts to nature and the pods. It can manifest from creating offspring with non-waterfolk. Depending on the other parent, the podling could manifest several abilities. There have been known pairings with the following species. Many which have multiple forms like ourselves." Shapes lit up the walls. From the images, I could identify humans, dragons, unicorns, whales, dolphins, sharks, swans, turtles, octopi, squid, goblins, elementals, and some kind of demon.

"Advantages in physique and magic have been added to waterfolk over the years because of our diversified offspring. It is hypothesized that our serrated teeth likely came from sharks in our ancestry, while whales and dolphins contributed to our overall capacity for knowledge. From humans and unicorns, we likely gained our initial magical abilities. In addition, we've passed these traits to other species. We believe these blendings have benefited the pods and should be encouraged," the storyteller concluded.

I couldn't believe how much we'd lost in a relatively short time, and I wondered when our isolation had truly started. I looked at my hands. How many could I have helped over the years had I grown up with my magic instead of discovering it a quarter into my life?

"Aisling, how many more crystals are in the cavern?" I queried.

"Hundreds. They are not sorted by a system I recognize yet," Aisling whistled.

It was an enormous task for one person. "Once the council members have met, we should organize a group to help catalog and study the crystals. It's too bad there are only two platforms," I vocalized.

Phyris vocalized, "Maybe there are more platforms. Now that we know what to look for, protectors can see if there are others in the pod."

I nodded. "Thank you, Phyris. This knowledge should go out to the whole pod. Everyone should know our histories."

"Where did the crystals come from? I haven't seen any crystal deposits in the caves." Royce queried. No one answered. "And do the platforms record as well?" We all glanced at each other.

There were so many answers and more questions. Halic could have answered some of them if he stayed, though I doubt he would have helped.

"We can only hope that we'll find the answers we need in the hatchery," I vocalized.

STASIS

Royce

After the council met, things moved quickly. The protectors discovered that most of the pods' dwellings had some kind of playback device for the crystals. Aisling and Daako supervised, handing out a crystal to each residence. After each individual or group listened to their crystal, they returned to the feast hall and told the council what was on the crystal. The duo began their own filing system in a room near the feast hall, not only to keep track of what we'd found but to make it accessible for anyone that wanted the information.

The waterfolk quickly named it The Treasure. So far, it contained pod history and stories about surface dwelling species, some which were thought to be long dead or so few in number that people hadn't seen them in ages based on what I knew.

Old council records started appearing. Nothing of note at first. The recording method was new, and they sounded like they were having fun with it. They even recorded songs they had heard from taverns in the ports. The harmonies were much better than any surface dweller could manage.

Then a recorded census surfaced. It detailed the number of waterfolk from different pods, those that had stayed on land, and those that had moved to other parts of the Gulf or the ocean itself. It also listed the number of magic users, and the types were astounding compared to the pod's current numbers.

The census dwindled year over year when reports came back to the pods about surface dwellers capturing waterfolk. Other reports recorded that waterfolk were forced to lead surface dwellers back to pods. The discovered pods were magically bombed from the surface and many died in the attacks, which were concussive, using sound to destroy rather than communicate. Hundreds of years of traditions and histories would have been gone if these crystals hadn't existed.

According to the crystals, they put plans in place to protect the pods. The recordings talked about Logan, a relative of Troller's pod. The same one Halic told Troller about. He lived on land and had some kind of manifestation magic that would cause things to happen. It was said he could perform curses, blessings, and transformations with ease.

Logan was sought by his relatives and asked to come back to help the pods. His solution was masking their magical auras. Because of the disguised auras, they stopped going to the surface to read the auras of the eggs. After a few generations, it seemed the pods forgot they even had access to magic.

It was mentioned that Logan safeguarded much of the magical histories, though it didn't specifically say what he did with them. The assumption was that he might have helped hide the crystals, and that's why the pods moved to the birthing grounds.

I also remembered Troller talking about Halic disappearing into a place somewhere on the surface.

"Troller, could this recording reference the place you first saw Halic?"

"It's possible. Halic mentioned Logan's study. It might be where he taught himself so much, along with what he might have regained naturally by going to the surface."

"I wonder, are the auras still masked? Or was it only the generation Logan was part of?"

"That's a good question. But the only way to find out is if we took eggs to the surface. I don't know if that's a wise decision."

"But things have changed. Surface dwellers are no longer a threat." What was the point of everything we went through if the waterfolk were determined to remain isolated?

"Royce, I understand, but I'm not the only one on the council. We need to decide the correct action after Halic's betrayal. If one pod returns openly, it affects all the pods, whether they stay below or not. Additionally, it's one thing to risk adult waterfolk in small groups and quite another to risk hatchlings and complete exposure." He put his hand on my chest, and I relaxed somewhat, though I was still impatient with how things were proceeding. "There is more information here and a room full of eggs which need to be taken to the surface to hatch. When the council convenes next, I'll ask them to take up the topic."

"I know you're trying to do the right thing, and that takes time. I only wish folks weren't so stubborn." To let him know I understood, I put my hand over his.

"Patience, my love. This is a lot for them, as it was for me when I first returned to the surface. You remember, don't you?"

I nodded and gave him a quick kiss on the cheek before returning our attention to the individuals discussing the crystals.

When the last individual reported what they had heard or seen, we left the feast hall together. As we reached Troller's dwelling, something surfaced from a hiding place in the rocks. A shark darted out and quickly went for Troller. While he swam away, I maneuvered to confront it. One swift hit with my fluke to its nose seemed to deter it. Troller came back to my side as we watched the shark leave.

We went inside our dwelling, and I swam in circles, still amped after what happened. "Why am I so agitated? This is the first time I've felt this." I was concerned. I'd been in risky situations before, even with sharks. Why was this one different?

"You're a protector, Royce. When your mate or the pod is threatened, your body reacts accordingly," Troller sang to me in soft tones, which calmed me. "I'm not in danger any longer, and the pod is safe. Do you believe me?"

I nodded. "What would have happened if you were not here?"

He did not answer me directly. "Protectors are either able to overwhelm the danger and back down on their own, mostly from exhaustion, or they continue to throw themselves at the danger until they die."

"That's horrific."

"That's in defense of the pod. This part of the ocean is safe because the protectors make it so. Those that come back from an encounter swim straight to their mate to be calmed so they can safely be inside the pod again."

Halic's choice of me as Troller's guard took on a more ominous angle. "Do you think Halic planned to use me against you because I lacked mating marks?" Halic had no idea I was human as far as we knew, though we still didn't know the extent of his abilities.

"The idea crossed my mind. However, I suspected your surface dweller instincts would protect you somewhat, and we saw each other as mates long before we declared it. If you hadn't considered us mates, you wouldn't have reacted to my efforts to calm you." Troller wrapped his arms around me, and I mirrored him.

"Wait a moment," I purred. "You liked that I defended you. Not just liked it, but really liked it. I just felt your . . ."

I wasn't able to finish that tone. Troller kissed me with such intensity, I couldn't help but purr. When he stopped, he quietly hummed to me, "Do you want to see how one can calm their protector mates?"

I nodded, grateful for my protective instincts as Troller's fingers slipped into my pouch.

GUARDIANS

Troller

For someone born to the currents, I had lost track of how many current shifts occurred between the Yearend feast and our efforts to learn about our past. Our pod caves became the center of activity for all the surrounding pods. Many came from all over the Gulf waters to learn. Still, it left Royce and I some time to ourselves.

I un-wove my hair and watched, amused, as Royce cringed slightly, biting the head of a shrimp and quickly eating it. He repeated the same actions with each shrimp he ate.

"When we talked about your transformation potion, I worried I wouldn't be able to find enough for you to eat," I vocalized.

Royce smiled. "I became less picky as time went on. I like seaweed and kelp, but it doesn't have nearly enough protein." He held a white shrimp in his hand, then offered it to me.

I took it and ate it whole. It didn't bother me that it writhed on my tongue.

"I had little choice in food sources living in the protector spaces. Whatever they collectively brought in was what we all ate. I learned to bite the heads quickly, or my dinner swam away."

I made a soft trill after I swallowed. "You still grimace when you bite the heads."

"I know." He made a shy trill. "While I understand that it's much less traumatic for my food to have me bite their head in the right place, my human instincts want to use a knife."

"Or eat seaweed."

Royce shrugged. "But I've adapted, like you did when you came to the surface. We've learned a lot from each other since we've been together." He reached out his hand. I touched his palm with mine. Webbed fingers and claws made threading our fingers together more difficult, but we did it anyway, if only to remember.

I pointed to the woven reed container holding the shrimp. "Are you finished?" Royce nodded. I took the reed rope attached to the container and wove it back into place so the rest of the shrimp wouldn't escape, then secured it to the side of the dwelling wall where the current would flow through the container.

"Any word about your or Aisling's guardians?" Royce queried.

They sent queries out with visiting pods to discover what happened to them. If they were scared or in hiding, I could not blame them for being cautious. If what Phyris had vocalized was true about my own guardians, then it would take time for them to hear about what happened and return from the edges of the territories the pods claimed.

The surface considered parents and guardians similarly. Waterfolk had a lack of emphasis on being blood-related. The community supported offspring regardless of their origins. That was likely because raising podlings was a group effort, and podlings picked their guardians. While podlings often chose the ones that conceived them, sometimes they didn't. And sometimes the ones that conceived them were no longer living. As a result, podlings became attached to whoever they picked. It was a lifelong relationship, and no one ever questioned it. As all adults were responsible for podlings on some level, but being a guardian meant you committed to seeing to the care of specific podlings.

I shook my head, and my hair flowed around me. Royce picked up a coral comb, smoothed by use, as we floated to the moss-covered ceiling. Royce put his back to the ceiling and bent at his waist and knee joints while I angled myself so that my hair flowed across what would have been his lap in his surface form. I used my fins to rest against the lower part of his tail.

Royce brushed the strands and caught them up into the pieces he needed to braid my hair. "Did the council make a decision about the hatchlings?"

"There was a provisional agreement to test some eggs if we can find a safe place. Word is spreading among the pods to find a secluded cove or beach that other species are not using."

"What about the eggs in stasis?"

"The council does not want to remove them until we can do so safely. However, anyone who wishes to safeguard their egg can place it in the cavern. Many have moved their eggs there. It's much safer than the birthing fields and easier to defend."

With the cave-in cleared and the passage widened, protectors had less area to cover.

As Royce's deft hands continued to braid, I wondered when I might be able to braid his hair. There were already several braids in his beard, making it less abrasive. We often had to remove the objects Galaina's podlings would place in his beard. Royce started a small collection on a shelf in our cave and often wore several when we visited.

A whistle came to us on the current, and Royce twitched with recognition. "It's Phyris. He must have news."

"He's come a long way. Is he not staying with Galaina now?"

"He is. Maybe he's not alone?" Royce returned the whistle, and an eager one replied, indicating he had indeed brought news.

With my braid finished, Royce secured it with the same leather tie he'd given me so long ago. With a pat on my shoulder, we floated away from the ceiling to greet Phyris as he arrived.

"Friends, I'm happy to find you." Phyris looked at me. "Councilor Troller, your guardians have been located. And..." He was very excited by this news, more so than I thought he would be. "They have magic."

I looked at Royce, and he smiled. "Where are they, Phyris?"

"Fifteen leagues from our pod toward the mainland. The protectors on patrol heard it from the songs on the current. They sent someone to tell me as soon as they heard. We have directions if you want to investigate yourself."

We left as soon as we had a destination. Royce swam next to me easily. Very little passed between us until we found the beach Phyris had described.

As we approached, we went to the surface, and I called out to my guardians. There was no answering call or indication that they were there until Royce pointed at something along the sparse tree line.

"That looks like a shelter, Troller."

They had magic. Was it possible they left the water to keep themselves safe from their own pod?

"I'll go ashore and find out."

"Be careful, my love," Royce vocalized. I nodded, then turned to swim for shore. As my fluke touched the sandy bottom, I shifted to have better footing. Once out of the water, I covered my eyes to see if I recognized anything else near the poor shelter of shrub grass and palm leaves.

The further onto shore I went, the more I worried about my guardians. There was not much available for them to hide from the elements. A sharp whistle drew my attention. I turned toward the sound and noticed Royce had his arm raised. I acknowledged him with a wave and continued toward the shelter.

It was there I found my guardians asleep on some woven mats covering the ground. They looked peaceful, but recognized the foul smell of sickness and filth. Neither of them had my deep red hair. Merk had wavy black hair that reminded me of Royce's hair now that it was long. Jani had soft brown hair, though it looked dull in the dim light. They both looked very pale as they breathed shallowly.

"Merk, Jani, can you hear me?" I intoned as best I could with my surface vocal cords.

Merk woke first. "Troller? It's you!" His throat tried to vocalize, but the sounds were broken and barely understandable.

"Yes, it's me." As I moved closer, the foul smell grew stronger. I noticed they laid in feces. "Are you unwell?"

"Ate something." He took a deep breath and sighed. All this time, only to eat something that made them sick.

"Happened before, but Jani healed."

I nodded to Merk. Jani was still asleep. "Let me take you to the sea. It will help."

"Not safe, Troller."

"It is. I promise." I picked up Jani before Merk could protest and brought her to the water. Royce came as close as he could once he saw me.

"Royce, take her under and watch her shift. She's sick."

"What happens if she wakes? She doesn't know me," he vocalized.

"I have to retrieve my other guardian. They are both sick." I didn't wait for Royce's answer and went to retrieve Merk. I brought him to the water, and when I could swim, I shifted. Merk shifted as we sank under the surface. When he finished, I wished his ailment healed.

When we reached Royce and Jani, there was a great deal of shrieking from both individuals as Jani tried to fight Royce's help. Merk swam into the fray and caught Jani by her waist.

"Quiet, my love. We are safe. Troller is here," Merk vocalized.

"Troller?" Her gaze caught mine as she swam toward me. I opened my arms to hug her, then held my hands to her back and used my magic to cure whatever she hadn't managed to before she became ill.

She sighed and queried, "How did you find us?"

"Protectors throughout the pods are sharing information. Some knew your location and had stayed away from you since one of you showed signs of magic. When word returned to us about where you were, Royce and I came to explain that it's alright now. You don't have to hide any longer. Halic has fled, and the pods are slowly returning to the surface."

"I thought we wouldn't make it. We were so sick. I was too weak to heal us both. Thank you, Troller," Jani vocalized.

"What made you leave the water?" I queried while I held Jani to soothe her.

"We were outcasts already because you went to the surface. We feared Halic would catch us. So we decided that if you could survive on the surface, we could as well. We only returned when we couldn't easily find things to eat," Merk vocalized.

"Do you both have magic, then?" Royce queried.

They both nodded. "Jani can heal almost anything, and I can stun things like an eel! Watch."

Merk's hands lit up with a white-blue glow. Dots formed on his hands and went up his arms until a larger fish swam past him, attracted to the glow. He reached out and barely touched the fish. It curled, then leaned to its side and floated toward the surface. Merk caught it by the tail before the tide took it. "Look, still breathing! It astonished me the first time I did it. I stunned an entire bed of clams, and they all opened with ease."

I released Jani, and she returned to Merk's side. They glanced between Royce and me before I reached out to take Royce's hand.

"I would like to introduce you to my mate." I gestured to my guardians. "Royce, this is Merk and Jani, my guardians." I vocalized. Royce worked to remain calm as my guardians approached. I tried not to trill as he held reasonably still while my guardians circled him like sharks.

"Is he a protector?" Merk queried.

"After a fashion. Royce is from the surface. When I met him, he was captain of a boat, and he very much protected his crew," I vocalized.

"What kind of boat? Where is your crew? Are they with you?" Jani queried as she eyed Royce's beard.

"A fishing boat," Royce explained. "No, they are still on the surface."

"How did you end up here, as one of us?" Merk looked at me and then at Royce.

"My guardians and Troller had a potion made that transformed me. I can't leave the water, or it would break the magic."

Jani clicked and reached for Royce's hand. She touched him gently, maybe trying to find out how the potion had worked. "So this isn't permanent. Will you leave or will you stay?"

Royce shook his head. "This is where I belong, with Troller."

I interceded at that point and looped an arm through Royce's, hooking his elbow. "Come with us back to the pod. You don't have to live out here alone any longer unless you prefer it."

"Are you sure it's alright, Troller?" Merk queried.

"I am very sure. And others will be interested in your gifts, including Aisling and Daako, who are our new knowledge keepers."

"Knowledge keepers?" Jani was curious. "What knowledge?"

She and Merk swam with us, and we told them about the changes since they left. It overjoyed them that the pods were thriving.

"How about your time on the surface?" Royce queried.

"It wasn't so bad," Merk vocalized. "Though eating with blunted teeth was difficult."

Royce smiled. "There are things that can make it easier and safer. I can teach you if you ever want to return."

"Thank you, but no," Merk clicked. "The water is our proper place."

Royce looked disappointed, but he let it drop. I smiled at him for his efforts. Like everything else, it would take time for them to adjust. The surface was the least of their concerns.

Their original dwelling, which was close to where Royce and I stayed, was still empty. The pod had not filled it because of superstitions. Not enough time had passed to assume that my guardians would not return.

Curious, I queried my guardians before we left them to their rest. "Was the beach you lived on inhabited?"

Merk shook his head. "We'd only been there a little while, and we were the only ones there besides sea birds and shelled creatures." I nodded and gave Royce a quick smile as we hugged my guardians one more time before leaving them.

When Royce and I returned to our dwelling, we ate the rest of the shrimp and then gently floated to the ceiling. We spooned, as Royce called it.

"Your guardians are nice," Royce clicked.

"I think yours would like them as well," I responded.

Royce vocalized his agreement. "Maybe someday they can meet."

"Perhaps, my love. Perhaps."

I smiled at the thought. They would certainly enjoy talking with each other and exchanging stories of our childhoods. Royce's would be a bit more interesting, to be sure, but then again, you didn't meet waterfolk every day. Though I might be underestimating the limits of Leo and Ben's ability to gather information.

SAFE HARBOR

ROYCE

After Troller's parents returned, several protectors were asked to venture to the beach that Merk and Jani had lived on. The goal was to find out if the place would be safe for the pod to let surface-oriented eggs hatch.

Phyris led the team himself. When he returned, he was happy to report the good news. "We've spent two turns above water. Nothing harmed us. Even the sea birds were friendly. I don't think they have seen many surface dwellers or waterfolk, and it's my recommendation is that we move the hatchlings in stasis there and leave a watch over them," Phyris vocalized.

The council members nodded. Troller was happy as well. "This will also allow us to find out if Logan permanently muted our auras. If so, then we'll determine another method to help these hatchlings with their abilities," Troller vocalized.

A group of protectors and guardians, all with some magical skill to help on the surface, took ten eggs from the hatchery to the beach. The act of moving the hatchlings broke the stasis spell they were under. Stasis spells, as we learned, worked if you didn't move whatever you cast it on. It was the only way the eggs in the hatchery had survived.

Those eager to serve as guardians to the new podlings waited on land and in the sea. From the histories the crystals gave us, podlings were given a choice at birth, allowing their instincts to choose which environment they wanted to acclimate to first.

Troller and I talked about our future once the council had decided on a course of action.

"Royce?" he queried as he rested in my arms on our moss ceiling with his head on my shoulder.

"Yes, my love."

"Are we ready to be guardians?" I turned my head to see his face. The bioluminescence was enough to see the smile that slowly formed.

"I was hoping you would ask. I would love to be a guardian with you, Troller."

"Truly?"

"I would see it as the greatest honor and achievement of my life to help you raise the next generation of waterfolk."

Troller trilled softly, "That was very formal."

"It was a solemn declaration. I wasn't able to propose to you, so this moment seemed like the next best thing." I reached to brush the back of my hand over his face.

His hand caught mine. "I am honored by you, my love."

We knew the podlings might not select us this time. Sometimes it took several hatches before podlings selected someone to be their guardian.

It took another five months before signs of life appeared on the beach. It was late in the Gulf current cycle when the hatching started. They placed torches on the beach to keep watch. The podlings clawed their way out of their protective shells to whistles and trills in the water and along the beach. They all emerged in their surface form, crawling quickly in a direction they had chosen. The visible clues that marked them as waterfolk were their sharp nails and pure black irises.

Two crawled toward those waiting on the beach while the other eight headed for the water. Once they submerged, they shifted into miniature versions of adult waterfolk, complete with fins, flukes, and gills. They quickly swam toward the waiting group of adults.

It was magical. Something like watching sea turtles emerge and make a break for it. They made noises and swam about while the adults purred and cooed at the podlings.

While we watched, a podling with red hair swam up to Troller. They moved around his head, then reached for his braids and played with them for a moment. The podling moved from Troller's hair to his shoulder, then slid a tiny, clawed hand down Troller's arm into his waiting, open hand. When the podling looked at us, they swam themselves into Troller's chest and stayed. I purred and touched Troller's back as he wrapped his arms around the podling.

As we moved away from the group with the podling in Troller's arms, I felt something latch onto my back and then claw their way to my neck. They wrapped their tiny arms around me and vibrated as they pressed into my back. I looked at Troller, my excitement and surprise making my stomach doing flips. Troller being chosen first seemed clear to me, but to have a podling choose me was an unexpected surprise.

I made a purring noise to calm them. The podling loosened their grip on my neck and eventually swam around to my chest. I tried to calm them even though their tiny claws dug in and the pain made me wince. Troller cooed to the small brown-haired podling, and they relaxed, eventually easing up on their claws. I wrapped my arms around them, and we left the group of guardians to wait for the other podlings to choose.

After all the podlings were safe with their guardians, the adults gathered food and celebrated with a feast. Another current shift after the hatching saw us on our way back to our dwelling with very sleepy podlings.

I checked the sling around my neck to ensure the podling was safe. Galaina had taught everyone how to make the slings out of reeds and seaweed during the feast. When Troller noticed, he smiled at me. "Royce, our podling is fine. Your weaving is sound."

We continued to swim, and a thought occurred to me. "Is it wrong to want to share this with my family?"

"No, my love. It's never wrong to want to share happiness."

"Do you think we could?"

"Yes. And I would have been surprised if you hadn't asked. It's time we let your family know you are safe and loved." I kissed Troller as our two podlings snuggled into their slings.

When we reached our dwelling, we ate and then slept together with the two podlings between us to keep them safe.

My parents were going to flip when they found out. That happy thought made me smile before I drifted off to sleep.

TRAPS

Troller

As soon as we could, we started our journey back to where we began. Brizo and Davit were fast learners. We had yet to test their ability to shift back to their surface form, but I was prepared to leave the water with them when the time came. Royce would stay in the water to protect them and keep himself from shifting.

There were many things I loved about my mate. His ability to navigate, even underwater, was definitely one of them. He even remembered fishing lanes with traps like the ones we used on his boat. Royce figured as long as we didn't take from the same pots twice, the fishers wouldn't know the difference.

We were several days along the journey back to the port in Galveston, taking our time and allowing our podlings to explore. It was our first family outing, as the surface dwellers would say. Royce and I were pleased with how curious our podlings were about everything. We delighted in their energy and marveled at their growth.

As Brizo and I were finishing our fish, Davit swam around us as they played in the small currents they found. Royce whistled as he pulled one more fish from a different pot and closed it before too many others could escape. "We should move on. I hear a boat heading in this direction. It's probably here to pick up the traps."

I clicked in response. "We're done, my love." I turned toward our redhead. "Agreed, Brizo?" I smiled at them, and they trilled back, pleased and full. I offered their sling to them, and Brizo swam in as I looped my arms through and slipped them onto my back. The podling snuggled up to me and covered themselves in my braids.

Royce chased Davit. I trilled as I watched them. Our Davit was fast and liked to frustrate us. It didn't matter who pursued them. They would rather swim than be carried, even though they were still slower at distances because of their size.

"Let them follow, Royce," I clicked.

Royce clicked back in agreement, then clicked at Davit, which got the podling's attention. "Follow us."

The podling zoomed past Royce and trilled agreement. Royce shook his head and caught up with me. "There's always one in the family."

I trilled, "Were you difficult, Royce?"

"No, but my cousin Daisy was. Her mother was the crowned princess. She was third in line for the throne and never let any of the rest of us lower children forget it."

The boat engines grew closer. I whistled for Davit, but there was no response. So I whistled again and looked around. I felt Brizo move in their sling. Royce and I both whistled, but neither of us saw the podling.

We were far enough away from the boat ourselves that we were sure they couldn't see us, but I grew more worried the longer we didn't see Davit.

We kept whistling without a response until we heard a piercing scream of alarm. Royce and I looked around, and he zeroed in on it before I did. He moved fast as we watched the trap, with Davit in it, rise through the water at a rapid pace.

I swam after them and watched as Royce grabbed the trap as it breached the water. I swam to the surface. Both Royce and Davit shifted to their surface forms. Davit's cry turned from a piercing scream to a baby's wail, which was no less disturbing because of what was happening.

The fishermen on board stared at Royce as he clawed the trap open, grabbed our screaming podling, then dove back into the water with Davit. I swam to Royce, grabbed his arm, and swam us away from the boat as fast as I could. Davit shifted back, but Royce was human. Once we were far enough from the ship, I brought us all up to the surface so Royce could breathe.

Royce coughed and treaded water as Davit vibrated with emotions and clung to Royce, drawing blood with his claws. I held out Davit's sling and coaxed them into it, then put it on my front. Royce worried me. He did not look well.

"Troller, I'm sorry," he said. I hadn't heard his human voice in a long time. He moaned in his misery, knowing what he had lost. I shifted to tread water with him, to speak with him.

"Shh, my love, you have nothing to be sorry for. You saved Davit's life."

"I was so scared, Troller. I didn't think. All this time away, and after everything we've done to defend them, I don't trust surface dwellers, not with our child."

"It's alright, my love, it's alright." I drew Royce to me as much as I could, still mindful of Davit.

"Troller, you have to go. Go back to the pod. It might take you a few days . . ."

"No, Royce. I'm not leaving you."

"In this form, I'm dead in a day or two from hypothermia, even if the water is warm right now. I can't maintain my body heat. If I'm lucky, a boat might come by and rescue me."

"I will stay until then." I kissed him, and he cried as he kissed me hard, conveying his sorrow. While we waited, I shifted back to keep us warm. The boat never came back. No boat came.

By the second day, the podlings screeched their distress at Royce, and he held them with me as best he could. He shivered until his shivers became full body tremors and his teeth clattered together.

"Troller, promise me you'll take them home. Go home. The pod isn't more than three days . . ." I shook my head. I would have shifted, except I was the only warmth he had. "Troller. You should go now. Go before they see."

He kissed each podling on the forehead, and they screamed. I vocalized my distress with them. I knew he was right, but I couldn't leave him to die alone.

"Before I met you, I wouldn't have ever imagined our life. Or a life with children. You gave me that. You, my love, my partner, gave me purpose. I love you, Troller. Please. Please go. Before . . ." He took several deep breaths that were hampered by the waves.

He slipped under the surface as a spasm forced him to let go of me. I dove for him as air bubbled out of his mouth. When I reached him, I breathed for him, as I had done once so long ago. Our podlings vibrated and screamed their distressed vocalizations. I poured my will and hope into Royce. Mentally begging him to stay. Wishing he was truly a waterfolk. I imagined him in the waterfolk form I knew so well.

I vocalized all my pain as I held onto Royce and breathed for him. His body became weaker as we sank further below the surface. I closed my eyes and knew Royce was right. That I should have left before this. I did not want to see his last moments. His organs would shut down, and even my ability to breathe for him would no longer matter. I closed my eyes and saw his waterfolk form. I remembered how he held me, the caress of his hands, the strength in his arms, the powerful fluke he used to defend me. Each detail I brought to mind as I tried to breathe for him. When the desire and hope to see him in that form again became too much, I made a wish and poured every bit of my magic into it.

It wasn't until I felt the water growing warmer that I opened my eyes to see Royce, in his waterfolk form, swimming us back toward the surface.

"Are we dead?" That seemed like the only explanation. The podlings were quiet for a moment until Royce trilled at them. They trilled their happiness in return.

"You didn't listen to me," he clicked. Our podlings wormed their way out of their slings and clung to him. I did, too, as he maneuvered us toward our original heading. I trilled my pleasure at him.

"If I had, you would not be here."

"And you wonder where Davit gets it from," Royce trilled. He kissed me and our podlings as he continued to swim. I wondered at his strength. Had my abilities given that to him as well?

It didn't matter. Royce was safe. I trilled with joy and happiness, and so did the podlings.

Royce found a small cave, and we sheltered in it for a time. We caught fish, ate seaweed, and rested. We watched the podlings swim, making sure they were not too far from us.

"I'm confused," I vocalized.

"About what, my love?" Royce queried.

"You were dying. I felt your heart slow, even as I breathed for you."

"I'm pretty sure it stopped, actually," he vocalized.

I whistled my shock, and it made the podlings come back toward us even though they were playing.

Royce continued, "My last thought. My last breath was wishing I could be with you and our podlings. I wanted to stay, Troller, more than anything. Then a kind of heat shot through me. I thought my nerve endings were trying to cope with my body shutting down. Instead, I think it was something you did. We were lit up like lightning. I felt my body shift back, and you went limp in my arms. The podlings clung to you while I swam us back to warmer water."

Davit swam to Royce and snuggled into his chest while Brizo came to me and nuzzled their way into my braids.

"I wished for you to be a waterfolk. With my whole being. I had dreams about it once, that a kiss would change you. It seemed like a fantasy, except now it's not." I smiled. "But I'll accept this reality because the alternative is more than I want to contemplate."

Royce trilled, and the podlings mimicked him. I moved with Brizo and curled up with Royce and Davit. We slept until the current changed again, then we ventured out for food as a family. When Davit clung to Royce less, we knew it was time to move on.

"Promise not to scare me like that again, my love," I vocalized.

"I'll try, but with these two, it will be extremely hard to keep that promise."

We trilled together, and the podlings joined in as we continued our journey toward our first stop: Royce's old boat.

OLD FRIENDS

ROYCE

When my family and I swam into the port where I knew the boat docked regularly, I was warier than when I'd left over two years ago. I had Davit in their sling on my back and Troller had Brizo. The podlings were cooing softly as they watched the fish dart around.

The sun was setting, and either the crew and Pete would be ashore for the night or cleaning up. That was if Pete even kept the boat. I didn't have any right to expect things would be the same. Especially since the last time I'd seen him, I'd left him tranquilized in my bed.

Aire Apparent, now Pete's ship was docked in its usual place. It looked like the cabin lights were on. Maybe Pete left them on, or he was about to leave. Or he sold the boat to someone else. I shook my head at the circular nature of my thoughts and swam toward it.

"You and the podlings should stay here in case Pete isn't onboard."

"Alright, my love. Be careful," Troller vocalized. I kissed him, then kissed Brizo and Davit on their foreheads and purred at them. They purred back. I smiled and swam to the end of the dock where the gangplank met the shore. I pulled myself up and sat while I shifted slowly. I hadn't realized how difficult it would be to have legs and feet again.

I used the railing along the dock, then again along the gangplank to get myself onto the deck. Once aboard, I sat down on a box of stowed gear to catch my breath and let the pins and needles ease out of my limbs a bit.

The person who walked out onto deck wasn't who I expected, but it was a familiar face.

"Hello Kristy." My voice sounded rough, but understandable. She jumped halfway to the moon. I hadn't meant to startle her. She turned slowly to look at me, her dark brown eyes wide with emotion, her hand on her chest. She looked good. Her hair was in tight braids against her head. I wondered if she and Troller had ever talked about braiding or weaving hair.

Once she got a good look at me and caught her breath, her eyes lit with recognition. "Royce?"

"Yeah." I smiled and blushed. It's not like I usually walked around my boat nude, but here I was in front of a former employee, and hopefully still a friend, naked.

She looked at me and smiled. "So you're not dead."

"Seems that way, though it's not for lack of trying."

She laughed. "Pete's going to lose his shit when he sees you. You practically look like Poseidon himself, with your braids and bits of shell in your beard."

I chuckled because she wasn't wrong. "Speaking of, where *is* Pete, Kristy?"

"He's home with Marcy and their kid."

I covered my face to keep the tears from being too obvious. I hadn't realized how much I'd missed my best friend and almost didn't hear Kristy as she continued to talk.

"When you left, he tried to run the boat, but his heart wasn't in it without you. He made me captain, and I took on a crew and ran the boat for him. We've done alright, but even with what you left him, he's struggling with all of it. Including the fact that he lost two friends."

I held in a sigh. "He didn't lose us." He knew where I went. Though I suppose after all this time and not a word whether we were okay would make anyone doubt.

"You've been gone for a while, Royce. You tranqed him and took off with barely a note. He had to break the news to your parents. They were devastated, though they basically adopted Pete and Marcy. You should see the presents they send, especially for the kid."

"What's their kid's name?"

"Rory."

The emotions I'd been holding back came for me like a tidal wave. *Fuck, Pete.* Kristy approached and put a hand on my shoulder. I wiped my eyes and nose, then took a deep inhale and let it out.

"Do you want me to call him?"

I nodded. Kristy turned to go into the cabin area, and I called back to her. "I'm not the only one here, Kristy. Ask him to bring some of his clothes and anything that might fit me. Also, maybe some of his kid's outfits." She looked at me with a curious expression, but nodded.

When Pete showed up making enough noise to be his own one-man band, I smiled, and so did Troller, as Pete yelled at the boat from the gangway.

"Kristy, if this is some elaborate prank by the guys at the bar, I'm going to dock your pay," Pete said, juggling a large duffle bag while he came onboard.

Kristy stood there with Troller, me, and our two kids. All of us were wrapped in the largest towels she could find.

"No prank, Pete, I swear," Kristy said as Pete finally dropped the large bag and saw who was on his boat.

"Hi, Pete."

"Royce?" Pete stood there a little dazed, and then a smile spread over his face as he looked between Troller and me, then our children. "You found him."

I nodded. "Come meet your godchildren." Pete walked over and smiled as he reached a hand toward Davit, who grabbed it immediately. "This is Davit, and that is Brizo."

Pete wiped his face. "You have kids." I nodded again. "Royce." He turned to my mate. "Troller." He sighed. "It's really good to see you both."

I pulled him in for a hug. He gave me one, then let go and hugged Troller. He cleared his throat and swiped a hand over his face to dry his tears. "I brought clothes. And we can do a maintenance week with the boat so you can stay here. I'll figure out how to do payroll for the crew. Oh shit, Royce, you need to see Marcy and Rory."

"Rory?" Troller asked as he glanced at us.

"Yeah, my daughter. Marcy is going to flip. Oh wow, and so are your parents! Royce, you have to call them. They'll want to know you're alright. Troller too. They really missed you both."

"One thing at a time, Pete." He nodded. "How about we start with clothes?"

"Oh right, shit. Yeah, that makes sense."

Kristy piped up then. "You can use the captain's cabin to change."

My old room was decorated differently. Kristy had posters of punk-electronic music bands and festivals, along with her certifications and licenses to run the boat. The foldaway was still there. I pulled it down, and we swaddled Brizo and Davit in fresh towels. Shifting to their surface forms had worn them out.

Once we had them settled, I undid Troller's braids so he could wash his hair. "How are you with all of this?" I asked.

"It's not as overwhelming as last time. We have family here. That makes all the difference."

"It does." I kissed his shoulder and finished unbraiding his hair. We switched places so he could unbraid mine. I hadn't realized how long my hair was until he'd finished. He played with it for a moment or two. "Do you like it?" I asked.

"Yes," he said with a low tone in his voice that half sounded like the purr he made underwater. "If I had a brush, I'd brush it for you."

"Maybe we can borrow one from Pete or Kristy." Troller hummed slightly as he swept my hair to the side and kissed the back of my neck.

"It's unfortunate that we haven't had time for ourselves." He was right. With the podlings as small as they were, anything other than sleepy kisses had been out of the question.

"Maybe we could talk Pete and Marcy into babysitting for an evening."

Troller leaned down to kiss me, and I thoroughly enjoyed it until he pulled away, dropped his towel, and went into the bathroom to shower. "Tease," I said. I heard his soft laughter as he turned on the water.

Kristy insisted we take the captain's cabin. She grabbed a few of her things and moved back into the crew quarters. "The soundproofing spell still works. Should help the kids sleep. Extra linens for the foldaway are in the usual place," she said. We were grateful that she let us displace her so suddenly. Troller and I curled up on the bed with the podlings between us, much like he had in our cave, and passed out.

The next day, the complications of having our podlings out of the water became stark. There weren't convenient cleaning fish, and their bodily functions amused them way more than it amused us. We showered them off and wrapped them in clean towels, but Troller and I were clueless about how we could better contain their messes. And neither of us knew what food was appropriate for children out of the water that had previously subsisted on a fish and seaweed diet. Pete, to his credit, rescued us once again.

"How's it going?" Pete asked as he scrunched his nose. I looked up to see him at the door to the cabin, a bag on his shoulder. I frowned. He laughed. "That good, huh?"

"Well, we didn't anticipate some things. It has been messy," Troller said, and leaned over to coo at them. The podlings giggled. That sound alone lightened the mood a bit.

"I brought supplies," Pete offered as he came into the cabin. He dropped the bag on the floor and knelt to open it. "How old are they?"

"A couple of months," I said.

"Really?" Pete looked at them again. "They look like they are almost a year old."

"Podlings can swim shortly after hatching. They learn to catch their own food about a month after. We would have come sooner, but it was easier to teach them what they needed near the pod." Troller played with the podlings as we watched. "As hatchlings—that's what we call podlings before they leave their eggs—they grow large inside their shells so they can better survive the sea."

"That's amazing." Pete smiled as Troller picked up Davit, who made squawking noises. "Okay, so," Pete said as he dug into the bag. "I have diapers. They're not the magical fancy ones, but they are reusable, and they can collect a bit before you have to change them out."

Pete showed us a cloth that had a water-resistant side to keep the mess in, with elastic that ran along the outside to keep it a bit more contained. They worked to move the messes away from the baby's skin, but only for a few times. Then you had to change it and wash out the waste pouch. Pete showed us how they worked, and the kids tolerated them, though Davit kept pulling at theirs.

Pete also brought formula and a milk cereal. We moved to the galley and tried to have the kids eat, but neither was having it. So in a last-ditch effort to put something in their stomach, I went through the fridge, pulled out the jar of marmalade I found, and grabbed the bread.

I smeared a bit on the bread and tore a small piece off for Davit. Pete held Davit and watched as the child reached out for the bread and then shoved it into their mouth. Davit chewed, and we watched as their eyes opened wide and a small hand made a grabbing motion for more.

"That's a winner," Pete said. Brizo liked it as well. We fed them pieces of bread until they looked sleepy. "Looks like they take after one of their parents at least." Pete laughed as Troller's face lit up.

"I have definitely missed pastries," Troller said in a dreamy voice. I leaned over to kiss his forehead.

"Now that the babies are content, maybe I can swing by the fish market and pick up just-caught for them to eat later. Hopefully, it will be fresh enough."

"We can try it," Troller said. "Though we might have better luck with vegetables. I was rather fond of those."

Pete handed Davit back to me and then pulled a phone out of his pocket. "I kept this, and your parents helped me keep the number active, just in case." I swallowed hard seeing it and knew the last message I sent to my parents wouldn't have been enough. It was one of the few regrets I had when I'd made my decision to go after Troller.

When I opened the phone and checked the messages, there were responses over the whole time I was gone. They contained Leo and Ben's love and concern, along with their heartbreak and worry at not knowing where I was or if I was alright. Davit patted my face gently, and I realized I was crying. I kissed their cheek and smiled at them to ease their worry.

I looked up Leo's number and called it.

"Hello?" The sound of my father's voice almost broke me. I had missed them more than I realized.

"Hi, Papa."

"Royce?" I heard something rustle, and Ben said "Huh" before Leo repeated something. "You're on speaker. Royce, sweetheart, where are you?"

"I'm on Pete's boat, in Galveston." My throat was tight with emotions. I tried to clear it, and Troller smoothly came up to me and took the phone. He put it on speaker and spoke to them.

"Hello, Royce's parents."

"Troller!" Ben said. "You're alright?"

"Yes, we're both well. We would like to visit."

"Absolutely," Leo said.

"This time, we'll come to you. Meet you somewhere close to your port," Ben said. "Is Pete there?"

"Yes, sir," Pete said with a smile.

"You tell our sons to stay there and stay with you, or there will be hell to pay," Ben said.

"Ben! Seriously?" We laughed and almost missed what Leo said next. "We'll send you coordinates like last time. We love you both, and we'll see you soon."

"See you soon. I love you too," I said.

"We love you too, son," said Leo. We ended in several goodbyes, and Troller ended the call and wrapped his free arm around me. The children were quiet while I cried into Troller's shoulder.

When I got myself back together, Pete had a smile on his face as bright as the sun. He rubbed his hands together, obviously excited. "Okay. Here's what we'll do next. Let's head into town, get some fish, and stop at Marcy's shop where Troller can eat his weight in pastries."

It was great to be home, and while I was happy, I also felt a longing to return to the sea.

"My love?" Troller looked at me. We were in the back seat of Pete and Marcy's vehicle, headed to town.

"Hmmm?"

"It will be alright. Everything will work out as it's supposed to. You'll see."

I nodded, then he kissed me. I hoped Troller was right. We were here together, and that's what mattered.

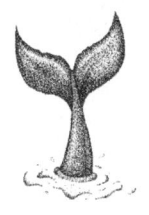

COMING HOME

TROLLER

As Royce and I adjusted to living on the surface again, we enjoyed our time with Pete, Marcy, and Rory. The children even played well together, sharing toys and not caring at all about their differences. I ate so many pastries that Royce was almost jealous.

"You keep moaning like that, you're going to wake up the podlings. And you're getting crumbs in the bed," Royce said as he brushed my hair. I was eating a late evening snack since Marcy had sent us back to the boat with an entire box of pastries for the third time that week.

"I see why Pete loves her. She's an excellent provider of pastries."

"I think he likes more than her pastries," Royce said in a playful voice as he kissed my neck, and I stifled a laugh.

We'd rigged small hammocks for the children and hung them from the ceiling of the captain's cabin. They were surprisingly easy to get the children in and out of, plus the light swaying of the boat rocked them to sleep pretty quickly. Royce and I finally had the bed to ourselves.

I put the rest of the pastry back in the box before turning to Royce to give him a gentle kiss.

"You taste like sugar," he whispered.

"Do you think we can be quiet?" I kissed him again and pushed him back onto the bed. He wrapped his arms around me and stifled a moan when I pressed my mating organ, hard and wanting, against his.

"By the sea, I hope so. I got supplies just in case."

I was amused that Royce was planning for this as much as I had. "I need you, my love."

Royce lifted himself up and kissed me with a fierce need that I felt as well. Our lips opened for each other, and his hand glided up under a pillow and produced a bottle of lube. In one swift move, I was on my back, and Royce trailed kisses down my neck, across my body, and over my hip.

His warm mouth kissed up my length and then engulfed it at the same time one lubed finger entered me. I slapped my hand over my mouth to keep myself quiet. I shook with the pent-up desires accumulated the last few months from stolen moments, quick couplings, affectionate kisses, and caresses. We had made as much time for each other as our responsibilities to our pod and our podlings allowed. I wasn't about to ruin my mate's very talented work with an ill-timed screech.

My other hand slid into Royce's hair, and when I got close, I tightened my fingers in his long tresses. He increased his efforts and added a second finger to quickly thrust with the first. With that, he brought me to a body-shaking release that left me panting hard.

I pulled him up my body and felt his thick length pressed into my hip as I kissed him profusely, tasting myself on his lips and in his mouth. The salt and mildly bitter taste remind me of our other home. It also reminded me that Royce was my home, and I was his. Wherever we were, as long as we were together, we were home.

I reached a hand between us as we continued to kiss and I stroked Royce. The softest groan slipped from his lips. We stopped for a moment, but all we heard were the deep breaths of sleeping podlings. I brought my leg up. Royce hooked it with his arm, bringing my knee to his shoulder, then positioned himself. I nodded as he slowly pushed into me. It was the sweetest burn I'd felt in a long while. When he had himself all the way inside of me, we stopped for a moment and kissed. Royce was shaking with need by the time we paused for a breath.

"My love," Royce said. I nodded again and put my hand on his hip. He started slowly, and I caressed his arms and shoulders. I pushed him a little, and he increased his pace.

I met his thrusts again with a soft "My love," falling from my lips as our flesh met in gentle slaps like water hitting the side of a boat. He bared his teeth and looked at me. I reached up and covered his mouth while I covered mine. His groan vibrated through my arm and into my chest as my moan joined his in muffled gratitude.

My arms wrapped around him as he collapsed to my chest, panting. His beard scratched my skin, and my fingers quickly found their way back into his long hair. We laid like that, joined only for a few moments, but it seemed like an eternity.

Royce cleaned up first, then I followed. We were excited for the next day. Royce's parents would be in the Gulf waiting for us. With the tension between us broken, we slept the rest of the night relatively peacefully until a chime let us know someone was at the door. Neither of us answered it.

The boat was moving by the time our children woke us. We joined Marcy and Rory in the galley as they ate a snack. Royce made slices of toast with jam and our children's favorite veggies.

"I'm going to join Pete for a bit," Royce said. I nodded. He kissed my head and took Brizo with him since they were done eating. I sighed softly, excited for the rest of the day. I watched as the two remaining children exchanged gibberish.

"Thank you for everything you've done to help us, and Pete," I told Marcy.

She shrugged. "Pete and Royce have been friends for a long time. You two and your kids are family. It's that simple."

I nodded. We were family, and it was that simple.

WE ARE FAMILY

ROYCE

I watched Pete flick a few switches to keep the boat on course as we made good time to the coordinates my parents had sent. I bounced Brizo on my hip as they made happy noises.

"You look like you slept well," Pete quipped.

"I did. So did the kids. Thanks for helping us with the hammocks. Those worked great."

"Happy to hear it. Marcy and I know what it's like to be in a small place with a kid. We still live above her shop to save money. We even splurged on a noise-canceling spell for Rory's crib. Sound can't get in, but we can hear if she fusses or wakes up. It's been a lifesaver." Pete smiled. "And a marriage saver."

"I'm glad for you two, seriously. And thank you again for letting us use the boat. I'm sure my parents will help with expenses."

"Royce, you're my friend, and so is Troller. I'd do anything for you both. But your parents' helping is a nice gesture." We laughed.

"Speaking of gestures," I said. "Why don't you and Marcy take the suite on my parent's yacht tonight? We'll watch the kids and keep them for the evening."

"Are you sure?"

"Yeah, since Troller and I will probably take a long swim tomorrow."

"Oh, I get it," he said with as much sarcasm in his voice as Pete could muster. "It's a bribe."

"Is it working?"

"Absolutely," Pete said as he grinned. I laughed, and Brizo laughed with me.

"Good. That's settled." I kissed Brizo's head, and they looked up at me with the same black irises Troller had. The same ones I had now as well. It caught me occasionally when I saw them in a mirror. I hoped my parents wouldn't be disappointed.

A few hours later, we were cruising into the coordinates. I heard Pete cut the engines and maneuver our boat close to the *Guardian*. We dropped anchor and let Ben maneuver the *Guardian* closer so we could tie off and bring a ladder to the deck. Leo dropped the fenders over the side and we worked together to bring the yacht to float alongside the *Aire Apparent*.

When they came up the ladder, their faces were everything to me. Leo approached me first and pulled me into a hug. "Ben and I missed you so much, Royce. So much." He and I cried together, and when Ben appeared next to us, Leo let go long enough for Ben to hug me with the same fierceness.

"Where's Troller?" Leo asked.

"Wait here a minute. I'll be right back," I said with a smile. I went to the galley and came back with Troller and our kids. Leo immediately cried again, and Ben hugged him as he looked at us.

"This is Brizo," I said of the small one in my arms, then nodded to Troller. "And that's Davit."

"Brizo, Davit, these are your grandparents." Troller clicked softly. He explained my parents were like Troller's guardians, Merk and Jani. They had known both of Troller's parents since the podlings came to live with us.

Leo dashed the tears from his face and held out his hands. "I need a grandbaby." I offered Brizo and Leo took them immediately. Ben noticed Pete, Marcy, and Rory too.

"I see you brought our other grandbaby too!" Ben said as he waved them over. "Come on, we have a ton of food on our boat. I hope everyone's hungry." Ben kissed Davit on the head and the child giggled. After a lot of hugging, we rigged the kids in slings so we could carry them down the ladder to spend the afternoon with my parents.

After a late lunch, the kids took a nap on the galley floor in the shade. Troller and I explained what had happened after the pod had taken Troller from the boat, our time with the pod, then returning to Galveston.

"Bloody hell, it's a damn fairytale." Leo drank more wine, while Ben was obviously trying to hide his emotional state. Hearing that I'd almost died to save Davit had not sat well with anyone, but I thought it was fair they knew.

I took Troller's hand. "We'd like to share the coordinates of the pod with all of you. We can work out a signal for you to send into the water to let us know you're visiting."

"That sounds easy enough," Leo said with a smile. "But why do I get the feeling there's more?" he asked.

"Because Troller and I need your help on behalf of our pod." I paused for a moment and looked at Troller. I had never asked for anything like this before, and what I was about to ask for was what I would consider a miracle.

"We found a beach that has no other inhabitants. We want it for hatchlings that are developing their surface form first so they can hatch safely and their guardians can live with them on the surface for a time. We're hoping you could help us safeguard it somehow." I couldn't outright tell them to buy the land, but I knew my parents were resourceful.

"Would we get the chance to see our grandchildren more often?" Ben asked.

"I don't see why that wouldn't be possible regardless of whether you assist us in this endeavor or not," Troller said.

"Good. Then we'll figure it out. Even if we have to pay for it ourselves, we'll find a way to make it work," Leo said.

Turns out San José Island was privately owned and mostly uninhabited. Originally a hunting and fishing resort for a wealthy Texan, my parents, with the backing of the royal family, purchased the island, then lobbied to turn it into a nature preserve that included the waters directly over Troller's pod.

They marked twenty leagues around the island as protected habitat. No one could fish there without permission, nor could you take an unauthorized boat outside the designated path to the island itself.

After we built a few small cabins, my parents moved to the island. The media blip was minimal, and when photographers looking for a quick buck couldn't reach the island without going through official channels, they eventually gave up.

As we moved the hatchlings to the shore in small groups, Leo and Ben saw it as their duty and honor to make sure cabins were stocked for the new guardians that stayed with the shoreside podlings.

Leo became the designated ambassador to the Southern Gulf waterfolk pods, which were five pods total, including Trollers. He learned the pod's language and met council members. It gave him latitude to help the pods with surface matters, like ensuring the island would be held in trust and had funds to maintain it long after all of us passed on.

A few years went by, and our podlings were nearly independent of us. They often visited my parents or Troller's guardians on their own. As a result, Troller and I spent more time swimming together. In addition, Aisling and Daako joined the council, and more of the old traditions of aura celebrations and hatching feasts returned.

When an egg from the hatchery was found with a magical compass inside its nook, it made everyone wonder why or who could have left it there. We decided to be part of the guardian group with this special hatchling. Troller and I hoped to be guardians to a few more podlings before we were too old to care for them.

Everyone knew the podling by the odd-shaped birthmark on their back, which appeared to be dorsal fin. Along with the red hue to their scales, it marked them as unique among the Southern Gulf pods. The egg also gave off a brownish aura, which was rare too. Once the podlings hit the water, the compass podling swam directly to us. We smiled as the small thing cooed in Troller's arms. It didn't claw or nuzzle, and their eyes watched everything with great interest.

We were about to leave with the podling when Daako swam to meet us. "You'll want this." He handed me the compass. "I couldn't find anything about it in the archives. But, by rights, it belongs to the podling."

I looped it around the podling's neck. The podling played with the object while we vocalized with Daako.

"Our thanks, Daako," Troller vocalized.

"Have you picked a name yet?"

"Benjamin. After my guardian," I clicked. Daako nodded again. Aisling swam up next to him, belly round with their own egg.

"Not much longer, hmm?" Troller queried.

Aisling shook her head. "No, and I'll be glad. We are ready to be guardians. I know this one will be loved by whoever they swim to." She passed a hand over her swollen belly as Daako kissed her forehead.

Daako smiled. "We are truly blessed."

"We'll be here for the aura celebration and the hatching feast," I vocalized.

"I hope so," Aisling trilled. The pair bid farewell and swam toward the other guardians holding their podlings.

"It's been a good day. We should find Brizo and Davit to let them see their new sibling," Troller vocalized.

"Maybe we could take them ashore to visit Leo and Ben, too." I cooed softly to the podling, and they purred as they played with the compass.

"I love you, Royce."

I moved closer to Troller and kissed him. "I love you too, Troller."

EPILOGUE OF PETE

ROYCE

Three Years Later

Pete, Marcy, and Rory came for a visit. My parents, as always, immediately scooped up Rory and took her to play with the island podlings. The island had grown into a small village where everyone could learn about the surface and magic and still swim home by supper. Guardians took turns teaching topics, and Ben made sure that the island could access the internet from a telecoms package he had built.

It was the best life, and I didn't regret leaving my boat for it. Kristy was a great captain and even better with the business. Pete eventually sold it to her. Marcy's pastry shop was expanding, and so was their family. This would be their last vacation before Marcy had their second child.

"Time flies and all that," said Pete right before he took a drink of his beer after catching us up on their current events. He'd brought several kinds of beer and a long list of wine requests from Leo. The island didn't make its own alcohol, so it was a nice treat to have while we sat on the beach.

"Yeah, it does, doesn't it?" I grinned at him. Marcy smiled, and so did Troller.

"Troller, can you help me up, then take me to find my wayward child?"

Troller glanced between Pete and me and gave me a pointed look, then smiled. "No kissing while we're gone." He was still slightly jealous. Later tonight, after we tucked our podlings in bed, that would be fun to play with.

"Does that mean we can kiss while you're here?" Pete egged him on and got a light swat from Marcy on his arm. "Ow." He laughed and grinned at her.

Troller and Marcy went off to find Rory, while Pete and I stared out at the water.

"That's still a thing, huh?" Pete asked.

"Oh yeah," I chuckled. "I like it when you visit. He gets feisty when you're around."

Pete laughed. "No, don't tell me. I don't need to know, seriously."

I laughed. "Don't tell me you're a prude, Pete."

"Nope, it's not that. Mostly it's because I have a decent imagination. It doesn't need help."

"You asked."

"I did, didn't I?" He chuckled and looked at the waves. "Speaking of decent imagination." He pulled out his phone, tapped an icon, and handed it to me.

"What's this?" I looked at the cover of a book. A waterfolk, much like Troller, was being held by a man about my size with a slight smile on his face. "The Fin and the Fury?"

"The title's pretentious, I know. It's a historical romance I've been working on. I'd like it if you and Troller could read it. Maybe tell me what you think?"

"Is this what you've been doing in your spare time?"

"Between the bakeries, Rory, Marcy, and the new kid on the way, writing is about the only thing I have that's my own. I do miss being on the boat sometimes."

Pete took a drink of his beer as I scrolled through the first chapter. "You've used our names."

"Easy enough to change in the next draft. I based most of the story on what you and Troller told us, so I used your names when I first started writing it."

I thought about it and shook my head. "No, don't change it. It's fiction and historical romance at that. If anyone ever asked, I'll say that we used to tell stories on the boat together. It's basically the truth. Not that I expect the media to find me all the way out here."

Pete grinned. "It is a bit of paradise, my friend."

"It is indeed." I glanced further down the beach. Troller and Marcy were on their way back, Rory between them and Benny plastered to Troller's side. Benny was three and way more curious about things than our other two younglings. Their dorsal fin had become more prominent each time they shifted, though in their surface form, it looked like a birthmark. Our only worry about our Benny was that they seemed to grow more anxious about it, especially around other podlings.

Troller showed Benny crystals that explained how the pods used to interact with other species, especially surface dwellers. In recent history, none of the pods had mated with other surface dwelling species. Troller and I had suspicions about how long

Benny might have been in stasis based on some of their physical traits and aura. For now, we were happy to see our families grow, and the pods take the first steps toward returning to the surface they had left behind.

IMPORTANT EVENTS THOUGH HISTORY

MAGICAL SPECIES PACT OF 1452

As trade and expansion became more prevalent, territorial wars and colonization became more commonplace. While harvesting parts of magical beings had always been unseemly, the trade and expansion of different empires pushed it into high gear. It was at this point that the Council of Elders, the wisest and oldest magical beings in Europe, came together to create the Magical Species Pact to protect magical beings or anyone that used magic. The pact made magical beings inert or non-magical upon death. If any part of the being was magical, it would render any magic that part or person carried inert. It effectively enforced tolerance between species that shared the same continent.

What they did not understand at the time was how this would affect beings with regenerative powers, such as phoenixes. Magical species that go through a cycle of renewal, such as phoenixes, have a duality of power as their death generates magic that causes a rebirth, allowing the individual to keep their magical abilities, whatever those were. There's been some side effects attributed to the pact, as phoenixes have reported issues with memory loss since its enactment.

Nor was death magic taken into account. Of the number of elders that were represented by the council, very few had any domain over the dead or undead. This was the loophole that allowed Joseph Florentine to thrive.

Necromantic War: 1873 to 1878 (the Necro War)

The major theater of war was in Europe and the Prussia Empire, though it spilled over into parts of the Russian Empire as well. Joseph Florentine had been an exceptional necromancer who rose to power in the mid-1800s. His platform centered upon allowing magic users the rights and freedoms to use magic as they pleased. He and his followers wanted to abolish the Magical Species Pact created by the Council of Elders to protect magic users. Florentine considered it the height of hubris that one of the most powerful groups of magical beings in Europe had forced magic users on that continent into the pact.

It took many magical species, including necromancers, vampires, and non-magical species (mostly humans) to fight off Florentine's forces.

About Author

M.L. Eaden works by day in the tech industry, but at night, she reads books, writes stories, throws axes, and is an avid gamer with a current addiction to Azul. Originally from the sunflower state, she migrated to one with a lone star (because it has more sun) and tries desperately to keep up with two adorable cattle dogs that still act like they are five years old instead of the seniors their vet says they are.

You can find M.L. Eaden on the following:

Author's Note

What can I say about Prince's Tide? This book baby had its difficulties. Even so, I absolutely adore this story. Originally it was an idea of a book mentioned in another book that is no longer on the internet. Someday that book will return in all it's glory, but I'm not completely sure if it will have the Easter egg that it originally had.

The character names from that idea didn't change, though. I even used the original title mentioned for Pete's book in the epilogue because I knew it was ridiculous but loved it all the same.

Fast forward a year, and some change, and we've arrive at this version. Different from the original I wrote, which had some problems. But not much different than the version I published to Tapas.

This edited and extended version is for all the readers that loved the original and wanted more. This is for the authors out there with the odd side projects that they write hoping that one day it might make it into someone's hands. This is the little love story that wouldn't leave me alone until the story was completely written.

Ultimately, its a story about finding the person that gets you, no matter what you wear or what form you show up in. It's about being your own person when everyone around you wants you to be or do something else. It's about found family and friends. It's about my favorite parts of being on the water, even the scary moments. It's a love letter to villains that do the wrong thing for the right reasons.

One of my favorite things about this book is the representation. Non-binary merfolk that choose their pronouns when they are older. A merman that prefers dresses when he's not working because they are more comfortable. A blonde haired dwarven lady that's bearded and flirty. Podlings and merfolk with natural afros. A gay, plus-sized captain who isn't the typical prince type. A bisexual first mate, writer, and best friend. An entrepreneurial Latina baker. A Black lesbian second mate. A non-binary crew member with fish scaled dyed hair. If you were able to pick all of that out about the characters and didn't feel like the representation was forced or token, then I did my job as a writer. I want to write stories about all of them. I might get to some day. But for now, they exist in this book, and I'm happy about that.

Finally, I'd like to thank D.T. Brandt for being one of the most awesome Beta readers for this book. He made some great suggestions I incorporated, especially the chapter where I expanded on Troller meeting the crew. If you haven't read his book *Something Between Us*, definitely check it out. It's on the Zon and KU. It's another queer centric romance between an aquatic based guy and his land based co-worker.

Until next time, happy reading!

M.L. Eaden

Original cover for Tapas. By Martin Whitmore

Also By M.L. Eaden

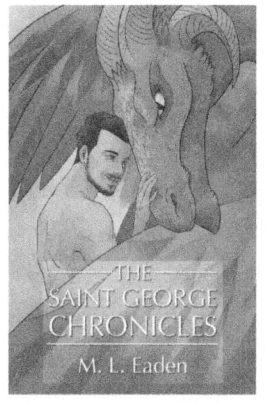

Gregor Lyndon became a public safety officer to help people. When Greg was thrown out of his family for being gay, he thought he left his family's legacy of canonized heroes that rescued maidens from dragons. What he can never get away from is his family's curse, which is the power to take down a dragon with one killing blow.

Xavior Brantley has lived a somewhat reckless life for a dragon. He's been an explorer, an investigator, traveled to parts of the world that humans and other beings have barely ventured. When he became bored with adventuring, he turned to public servant work. When he transfers to a precinct, Xavior doesn't realize his life was going to become a lot more interesting when he meets Greg and discovers the secret he's avoided facing for some time.

This is a spicy, yet slow burn, dragon shifter romance with a HFN ending. Content warnings are available in the front matter or at mleaden.com

During the height of the Necromancer War, Mason's fate was decided. While dealing with the transition from human to vampire, Mason finds work in the infected ward as a medic where she meets Ian. Not everyone survives to become a vampire and Ian becomes her mentor in all things undead.

Mason seeks Ian for help, though they haven't seen each other in over a century, after she rescues a young girl. The reunion isn't the stuff of fairytales. Ian has a new lover, Jason. And Dorothea, the girl Mason rescues, is more important than she realizes.

The more the group discovers, the more each answer unfolds into a plot to retaliate against the one person who can hold vampires accountable—The Envoy. Mason risks her undead life and relationship with Ian and Jason, to discover what's happened and return Dorothea to her family.

This is a spicy polyamory speculative fiction with a HFN. Content warnings available in the front matter or at mleaden.com

Other Books Supported By

Bitter and depressed after a bad breakup, Serafin moves towns to escape his old life, only to find when he arrives that his brand new home is haunted by an oddly handsome ghost.
Charming, confident, and mysterious, Darius is both alluring, and impenetrable.
As Serafin learns more and more about his ghostly inhabitant, he has to fight his feelings, but with every day that passes he finds it harder and harder.

The question always on his tongue:

"Could I ever love a ghost?"

An average woman's life is turned upside down when she's attacked by a serial killer and turned into a werewolf.

Sara Sheppard should be dead.

She has no idea how she survived the brutal attack and wants nothing more than to get back to her normal, boring life. But something—someone—is after her and she fears it will return to finish what it started.

Now she is faced with an impossible decision: live the rest of her short life in fear, or trust in a man defined by secrets. He appears to hold all the answers, yet those answers are even more unbelievable than her miraculous recovery.

Werewolves aren't real.

Or at least they weren't until she was bitten.

Made in the USA
Coppell, TX
27 October 2023